"Champagne it is," he said.

With a murmur of assent, the stewardess glided away.

"You're right," Dante said, looking directly at Connie. "It is something to celebrate. We've both gotten what we wanted. That's worth toasting."

A soft pop of a champagne cork came from the galley area, and then the stewardess was walking back with a tray carrying two gently fizzing glasses of champagne. She offered one to Connie with a perfunctory smile, then, with a much warmer smile, the other to Dante. She glided away again.

Dante held his glass out across the aisle.

"getting what we want," he said to Connie. He clinked his glass against hers, and took a mouthful of the beading liquid.

Connie took a sip of hers, feeling it effervesce in her mouth. Her eyes slid across to the man she had just married. Felt again that strange, irrelevant, impossible emotion well up within her—however utterly, totally, out of place it was.

Getting what we want—

Dante's words echoed in her head, and in their wake, came a sudden sweeping desolating thought...

That would never be true. Never *could* be true.

Julia James lives in England and adores the peaceful verdant countryside and the wild shores of Cornwall. She also loves the Mediterranean—so rich in myth and history, with its sunbaked landscapes and olive groves, ancient ruins and azure seas. "The perfect setting for romance!" she says. "Rivaled only by the lush tropical heat of the Caribbean—palms swaying by a silver-sand beach lapped by turquoise waters... What more could lovers want?"

Books by Julia James

Harlequin Presents

Billionaire's Mediterranean Proposal
Irresistible Bargain with the Greek
The Greek's Duty-Bound Royal Bride
The Greek's Penniless Cinderella
Cinderella in the Boss's Palazzo
Cinderella's Baby Confession
Destitute Until the Italian's Diamond
The Cost of Cinderella's Confession
Reclaimed by His Billion-Dollar Ring

Visit the Author Profile page
at Harlequin.com for more titles.

Julia James

CONTRACTED AS THE ITALIAN'S BRIDE

Recycling programs for this product may not exist in your area.

ISBN-13: 978-1-335-59295-8

Contracted as the Italian's Bride

Copyright © 2023 by Julia James

For questions and comments about the quality of this book, please contact us at CustomerService@Harlequin.com.

Harlequin Enterprises ULC
22 Adelaide St. West, 41st Floor
Toronto, Ontario M5H 4E3, Canada
www.Harlequin.com

Printed in U.S.A.

CONTRACTED AS THE ITALIAN'S BRIDE

For family carers everywhere—you know the good you do.

PROLOGUE

Dante Cavelli sat on a bar stool in the cocktail lounge of one of London's fanciest West End hotels, long fingers curved around the stem of his martini glass. He glanced at his watch—a slim, gold, ultra-expensive item—to check the time. She was running late.

He threw his glance out across the plush cocktail lounge. It was low-lit, with tables spaced out across its wide expanse, and in the corner was a white grand piano on which a female pianist was playing soft blues music. Dante's gaze rested on her for a moment. Blonde, very attractive, long hair curled appealingly around one shoulder. His thoughts flickered, then became rueful. No—out of the question.

He moved his gaze on, towards the entrance to the lounge, arched brows frowning over dark, long-lashed eyes. Lifting his glass, he took a mouthful of his drink, then put it down, his gaze still focussed on the entrance, fingertips lightly drumming a staccato beat on the bar's shiny surface.

Then they stilled. A woman was standing on the

threshold, and if the blonde pianist had caught his passing interest a moment ago then the woman in his eyeline right now did so completely. The change in lighting from the bright hotel foyer beyond to the more dimly lit cocktail lounge gave her a chiaroscuro effect as she stood there, framed in the entrance.

And what an effect...

Dante felt every Y chromosome in his body come alive.

It was her figure first of all—tightly sheathed in a cocktail dress of dark peacock-blue-green that moulded every centimetre of her oh-so-lush body, knee-length, skimming her shapely legs, which her high-heeled shoes extended in an enticing fashion. The fingers of one hand were folded around a clutch bag that matched the colour of her dress, and her other hand was lifted to just above her full, exquisitely moulded breasts as if—Dante's Y chromosomes gave another jolt—as if she was drawing breath. As if she was slightly nervous...

But what she had to be nervous about he had no notion. Not with a body like that.

As to her face...

Another slight frown formed between his brows. Poised as she was in the doorway, she was half in shadow, half not, which made it hard to see her features. He caught an impression of sculpted cheekbones, deep eyes, lush mouth. Her hair, glinting mahogany in the light, was swept into an updo that revealed her long, graceful neck, accentuated her delicate jawline. Quite enough to make him want to see more of her—all of her.

Then, just as he was mentally urging her to step forward, someone else entered the lounge, and perforce the woman had to move slightly to let him by. It allowed the full light from the overhead spot to fall on her, illuminating her clearly.

As it did, the breath froze in Dante's lungs.

And total shock detonated through him…

It can't be!

Because it couldn't be. It was just…impossible.

Non credo…

The words echoed numbly in his disbelieving brain.

CHAPTER ONE

Twelve months earlier

DANTE WAS DRIVING way too fast, especially for these country roads, his face set. His mood was vicious, just as it had been ever since the bombshell in his grandfather's will had exploded. His hands tightened over the wheel of the hire car, anger coursing through him.

Didn't I do everything he wanted me to? At his beck and call twenty-four hours a day. I gave him my total loyalty—met every demand he ever made of me.

And now his grandfather had done to him what he had—made that outrageous, pernicious demand in his will.

Fury seething, Dante glanced at his satnav. It showed he was nearing his destination.

A wedding.

The irony of it was without a scrap of humour. But it was where he would find the one man he needed now. His lawyer.

His old friend Rafaello Ranieri might be as smooth as burnished silk, but he knew his stuff. He damn well should, Dante thought grimly, given that Rafaello's law firm handled the affairs of half of Italy's richest families.

Dante, despite being in that elite company, had never needed Rafaello's professional services.

Until now.

He felt his black mood improve marginally. OK, so it had been a complete pain to chase Raf down to this back-of-nowhere country house wedding venue in the UK's West Country, where his friend was a guest of the Italian groom, but if anyone could find a way out of the trap he was in, surely Raf could.

But less than half an hour later Dante was staring—no, *glaring*—at his old friend, his face stark, his expression as furious, as disbelieving, as it had been when he'd read his grandfather's will.

'Raf, come on! There *has* to be an escape clause!'

Rafaello shrugged elegant shoulders in his expensive dinner jacket.

'He's made it crystal-clear. And watertight,' he repeated to Dante. A smile almost of amusement crossed the lawyer's saturnine face. 'So, tell me,' he asked, handing back the copy of Dante's grandfather's will, with a tinge of humour in his voice, 'who is going to be the lucky woman snapping up one of Italy's most eligible bachelors? So far you've only ever indulged in oh-so-fleeting affairs.'

Dante's eyes flashed darkly. 'Don't hang that one on me. I've never damn well had time for anything else, and you know it! No time for any kind of meaningful relationship.'

His friend lifted the glass of champagne he'd placed on a nearby pier table in the empty lounge they'd been shown into, well away from the wedding guests, so he could peruse the will.

'Well,' he mused, 'isn't that what your grandfather is seeking to rectify? To ensure you now form a permanent relationship. Or, of course,' he said, 'you could forego your inheritance.'

Something showed in Dante's face that was not just fury. 'I worked for that inheritance, Raf. I damn well *worked*! I gave my grandfather everything he ever wanted of me!'

There was frustration in his voice, but more than that. Hurt, bewilderment...

His grandfather had raised him from a boy—a boy whose own father had never worked a day in his life. Who had ended up crashing his car, killing himself and his wife in it. As for his mother—well, her idea of work had been to paint her nails and stress over which gown to wear to whatever party she was going to.

That was why, Dante knew, not without a stab of bitterness, his grandfather had insisted that a boy with such idle, self-entitled parents should understand that money did not grow on trees—it had to be made, by putting in hard work and long hours.

And that was just what Dante had done for the last dozen years, since leaving university with his first-class degree in economics and finance. Worked non-stop as his grandfather's deputy—and his eventual heir. That had been understood. Promised.

And now, instead, he'd been cheated of it.

'Dante, don't take it to heart so.' Raf's voice was not amused any longer, only sympathetic. 'Look, while the will is watertight, it may not be perpetually binding. He stipulates marriage as a condition for your inheritance, but...' he looked meaningfully at his grim-faced friend '...it doesn't stipulate a life-long marriage.'

Dante's eyes narrowed. He understood immediately what his friend was saying.

'What's the minimum term?' he asked bluntly.

Rafaello took a considering sip of champagne. 'Well, you must avoid any risk that the marriage might appear...artificial. That might well void the terms of the will. So I'd say, off the top of my head, it would probably be safe to consider a term of around two years.'

'*Two years? Dio*, I'll be nearly thirty-five by then. Looking at forty!'

Rafaello shrugged again, but sympathetically. 'Well, let's say eighteen months at the minimum, then. Could you stomach a marriage that brief?'

Dante glowered. 'Marrying,' he said bleakly, 'for any length of time at all, is the very last thing I want to do.' He looked at his friend. 'Raf, you knew my grandfather. He controlled my life while he was alive, telling me it was both my responsibility and my privilege to be the man to keep the company he founded going, given that my father was such a waste of space. And now,' he went on, the bitterness blatant, 'he's still trying to control me from the grave. Keep me chained…tied down. Allowing me no freedom even over my own damn personal life!'

Rafaello was frowning again, consideringly. 'Well, what if you found a woman who would make no demands on you? Who only wanted a marriage of convenience herself? An outward formality, nothing more, and for a limited period of time?'

'As if that's likely,' Dante growled.

Whether or not Raf's cynicism about Dante being one of Italy's most eligible bachelors was justified, he knew from his own necessarily fleeting affairs, snatched out of his punishing work schedule, that many females would snap at the chance of marrying him. But it wouldn't be some form of in-name-only marriage they would be after. They'd want the full cosying-up-for-ever-with-a-lavish-dress-allowance-and-a-baby-or-two-to-tie-him-down-with kind. Permanently.

The very thought was anathema to Dante. To be constrained—*imprisoned*, damn it—in marriage to a demanding wife every bit as much he had been by his grandfather's iron control…

But his friend was undeterred by Dante's rejection of his idea.

'I don't see why not. She might have reasons of her own for wanting marriage for a very limited period of time, and in name only—for having, in fact, very little to do with you. There would still have to be good reasons for it, though, so it didn't arouse suspicion and potentially breach the conditions of the will.'

Rafaello's ruminations did not impress Dante.

He gave a dismissive snort. 'And how do I find such an ultra-convenient bride?' he asked sarcastically.

'Who knows?' Rafaello said genially, placing an arm around Dante's tense shoulders and starting to guide him towards the hall, which was empty now as the wedding guests took their places for dinner. 'You might find her here tonight. So I think it would be a good idea for you to crash my friend's wedding…'

Another derisive snort from Dante was his only answer.

Connie was harassed. She always was at these events. Ideally, she wouldn't be here at all—she'd be at home with her grandmother. But apart from cleaning the two holiday cottages next to her grandmother's, the only work she could take on was in the evenings, when Mrs Bowen from across the way was happy to come over and sit with her grandmother.

And evening work meant either putting in a stint at the local pub in the village or, as tonight, up at the Big House—Clayton Hall—where another fancy wedding was taking place. Wedding work was always stressful, but it paid better than the pub, and she was in no position to turn money down. Especially now.

Connie's stomach pooled with cold dread. What on earth were they going to do, she and her grandmother? The cottage they'd rented for decades had recently been sold, and the new owner wanted to make it a holiday let, like the two next door, which would bring in far more money than a permanent tenant.

But where can we go?

The question circled in Connie's head, finding no answer. More and more landlords were turning their properties into lucrative holiday lets here in the West Country. She'd applied to the council, but had been told that local authority accommodation would mean a pokey flat in town. Even worse, they had suggested her grandmother going into a care home.

Now the cold in Connie's stomach felt like ice. Her heart squeezed painfully. No, she wouldn't put her grandmother in a home—and nor would she move her into an upstairs flat with no garden, in unfamiliar surroundings. People with dementia—the dread disease tightening its grip on her grandmother with every passing day—needed familiarity, or their distress only mounted.

Oh, please can she see out her days in the cottage that has been her home for all her adult life?

That was the heartfelt prayer Connie made every day—but it looked as if it was not going to be answered.

Because how could it be?

How could it possibly be?

She pushed through the service door into the now deserted hall, scooping up the used glasses left on side tables. Tray full, she hurried past the door leading off the hall just as it was yanked open and someone exited, careering right into her. She gave a shocked cry, the jolt unbalancing her level hold on the heavy tray, and half a dozen of the stacked empty glasses slid to the edge and plunged off, smashing on the tiled floor.

Another cry broke from her—dismay.

Simultaneously a voice exclaimed behind her. *'Accidenti!'*

It sounded angry.

She dropped down, placing the tray on the floor and frantically gathering up as much of the broken glass as she could see.

Suddenly there was another pair of hands doing likewise. *'Mi dispiace*—my apologies.'

It was the voice again, but not angry this time, merely impatient.

Connie glanced sideways. A pair of powerful thighs hit her eyeline, trouser material stretched taut, and she blinked and lifted her gaze slightly to take in the rest of him.

Her eyes widened. The man hunkering down beside her was, quite simply, out of this world. Dark hair, dark eyes and a face… Oh, a face that looked as if it should be on a movie screen! For one timeless moment she could only gaze, aware that her mouth was falling open and she had turned completely gormless. Then, with a mental start, she resumed gathering up the broken shards.

Another voice spoke—not impatiently, but rather with a drawling quality. Though it was hard to tell as Connie realised he was speaking Italian, so she had no idea what he was saying. The man with the movie star looks straightened, then said something back in Italian to the other man.

Connie grabbed the final shard of glass and got

to her feet, lifting the tray somewhat precariously as she did so.

'I'm so sorry,' she said automatically, her gaze anxious.

'It was not your fault,' the Italian movie star said. He glanced down at the floor at her feet. 'There is a fair amount of liquid from the glasses—you will need a mop, I think.'

Connie swallowed. 'Oh, yes—yes, of course. Um...'

She didn't know what to say, standing there flustered and nervous, knowing that her brain was in meltdown because a stunning man was speaking to her. The other one, whose looks were saturnine rather than drop-dead fabulous, was saying something—in English this time.

'A mop?' he prompted.

His tone was dismissive, like the look he gave her. She felt herself flush, shoulders hunching self-defensively, and fled towards the service door. She was used to dismissive looks and comments. Particularly from men.

And a man who looked like that would be even more likely to make them!

She frowned slightly. Except that it had been the other Italian who'd given her the usual kind of glance, not the one with the incredible movie star looks—the drop-dead gorgeous one who'd been so nice to her about the dropped tray and smashed glasses.

She gave a faint sigh and didn't know why. Then,

with a mental shake, she walked through the service door and went off to find a mop.

Dante glanced unenthusiastically around him at the other wedding guests as everyone tucked into the lavish wedding breakfast. Rafaello had had a quiet word with his friend the groom, and his English bride, and Dante was now included in their number to replace a no-show. Although he couldn't help thinking rather cynically that being young, wealthy and not exactly ugly meant his presence here was probably quite welcome.

'You can… What is that English expression…? *Case the joint*,' Rafaello said in his languid manner. 'See if any unattached females here meet your urgent requirements. I can already see that you are being eyed up as an object of new interest…' he added, with the same wry amusement.

His answer was an unamused scowl from Dante. Raf might be finding his predicament hilarious—damn him—but it wasn't him facing it!

How would he like having to lose his freedom—just when he thought he'd gained it?

Living his life under his grandfather's control had become increasingly chafing as the years had gone by, and, love him though he had—he'd been grateful for the stability of his upbringing when it would otherwise, courtesy of his feckless parents, have been chaotic and haphazard, spent mostly packed off out of his neglectful parents' way in boarding schools—Dante knew that his grandfather's unexpected and sudden death from a heart attack three months ago had also been a kind of release for him, harsh though it was to acknowledge it.

I felt I had finally got my life to myself—free to do whatever I wanted. No responsibilities. No answering to anyone else! Making my own decisions about my own life.

Of course he would still have the responsibility for taking on the running of Cavelli Finance—that was understood and accepted. Welcomed, even. He already had plans to develop his grandfather's business and take advantage of new opportunities for investment—especially in the field of green finance, which his highly conservative grandfather had obdurately blocked, despite all Dante's persuasive arguments.

But when it came to his personal life… Well, he'd thought he would finally be free to do whatever he wanted with it. Which was, he'd decided not settling down into marriage, or starting a family, but also not being anything like his own self-indulgent, party-loving parents had been either. There had to be a happy medium.

And now his grandfather had reached from beyond the grave to get his own way…

Frustration and anger roiled in him again, darkening his mood even more. He couldn't even drown it in alcohol—he was booked into a hotel in the local town, and the wedding venue was packed solid, so he needed to drive tonight. Besides, he wasn't in a mood to drown his frustrations. Only to let them feed upon themselves. Dark and brooding—and totally unsolvable.

* * *

Connie was hurrying down the long drive from the Hall towards the electronically controlled gates, head bowed, for it was starting to rain. The wedding party was still ongoing, but she'd made it clear to the catering manager she had to leave at eleven. She could not ask Mrs Bowen to stay any longer with her grandmother, and besides, Gran would need to be put to bed, not just doze in her armchair. Even though these days she hardly noticed what time it was.

A sigh escaped her. Oh, what were they going to do now that their home was going to be taken away from them? The problem went round and round in her head. Totally unsolvable.

Her tired feet stumbled slightly on the gravelled drive. She still had half a mile to walk down country lanes to reach the village, and she would need a torch once she was beyond these gates.

She'd just passed through the gates, which had opened to the exit code she'd been given, and was standing on the other side, fumbling for her torch in her handbag, when she heard a noisy car, accelerating fast. She saw the gates were starting to close, then was blinded by headlights approaching at speed. Presumably the driver wanted to make it through the gates while they were still wide enough, rather than slow down and wait to reopen them.

With a final roar the car made it through the narrowing gap, throwing up a slew of gravel, a little of which hit Connie in the legs as she lurched back instinctively to get away from the car. She gave a cry of shock, mixed with pain from the stinging gravel, and dropped her torch. Immediately she crouched down to find it, not registering that the speeding car had slowed to a halt and the driver's door was opening.

'Are you all right?'

The voice that spoke out of the darkness was sharp. And accented. And familiar.

Her head flew up. 'I dropped my torch,' she said.

He hunkered down beside her—the Italian wedding guest with the face of a movie star.

'Here,' he said, picking it up from the place it had rolled away to, holding it out to her.

'Er…thank you,' Connie said, clambering to her feet.

The drop-dead gorgeous man did the same. Light from the security lamps fell on his face, making his features even more arresting, and the rain created diamond drops in his dark hair and on his ridiculously long eyelashes.

The light also showed her he was frowning.

He said something in Italian, then in English. 'You're the waitress who dropped the glasses.'

'Yes,' said Connie. There wasn't much else to say.

His frown deepened. 'You have no umbrella,' he observed.

'Er…no,' said Connie.

She made to shuffle away. She was getting wetter and wetter and she needed to get home.

Suddenly she felt her arm taken.

'Get in the car,' he said. 'No, don't object—I'm getting wet too.'

He said something in Italian, which sounded condemning of English summertime weather, but he was simultaneously leading her towards his car, its headlights now cutting through the more heavily falling rain. He yanked open the passenger door, propelling her forward with his hand at the small of her back.

'No, really…please, it's quite all right.'

An expressive look came her way.

'It clearly is not "quite all right" at all,' he said stiffly. 'I will drive you home—it cannot be far if you were intending to walk.'

'Just into the village,' said Connie, collapsing into the car seat because it was easier than arguing.

It was a very plush seat, and a very plush car—the most expensive she'd ever been in, in her life. She sat back, hurriedly pulling at the seat belt as he got into the driving seat beside her, gunning the engine with a powerful roar.

She glanced sideways at him surreptitiously, feeling awkward and horrendously self-conscious about what was happening. In profile, the impact of his stunning good looks was just as jaw-dropping, bone-melting as full-face, and she jerked her head away lest he catch her looking at him. Gawping at him, in truth.

'Er…it's very kind of you to give me a lift,' she said, addressing him while staring rigidly out through the windscreen as the wipers slashed furiously to and fro.

'Do you start all your utterances with "er"?' came the pithy reply.

'Do I...?' she answered, flustered. 'Um... I suppose I'm just—well, a bit nervous.'

He expertly rounded a tight bend at a speed she was not comfortable with, but with which, she allowed, he seemed to cope very well.

'Nervous?' His voice changed and she almost heard the frown in it. 'I assure you, *signorina*, you are perfectly safe with me.'

Connie felt herself colour, was thankful that he could not see it. Of course she was perfectly safe with him. The very idea of anything otherwise...

His sort of females are like those ones at the wedding—designer frocks and killer heels and real jewellery, all groomed and coiffed and with long nails and perfect make-up. The total opposite of me...

Her rueful but resigned thoughts were interrupted. 'We are approaching the village. Where do you wish to be dropped off?'

'It's just past the church. A little row of cottages. Gran's is the last one.'

'Gran?'

'Yes, I live there with my grandmother. At least for now.' She could not stop something entering her voice that had no business being there in these bizarre circumstances. 'We have to move out soon,' she said bleakly.

The car was coming up to the church, with its ancient graveyard and the small terrace of cottages beside it.

'That's a shame,' came the voice of the fabulous

fantasy Italian. 'It looks very attractive—this whole little row.'

Even in the rain and the light from a solitary streetlight some way away the cottages were chocolate box pretty, with roses round the door and little front gardens with picket fences.

'Yes, the other two are holiday lets. The new owner wants Gran's to be one too. So we have to leave.'

Connie fumbled for the door, glancing back at him, ready to thank him for the lift and hoping her colour would not rise as she did so. That would be too embarrassing.

'That will be hard for her at her time of life. The elderly like familiarity,' she heard him say.

It seemed an odd thing to hear from someone like him, but she could not disagree.

'Especially when they have dementia,' she said. 'Anything new is horribly confusing for her. And besides...' she knew she sounded bleak '...nowhere else will be as nice as here. There's nothing available to rent privately that we can afford—everything is becoming holiday lets now. We've been offered an upper floor council flat in town, with no outside space, or Gran will have to go into a care home. I'm dreading it, but it has to be faced—there's just no way for us to stay here.'

She heard her voice tremble. What on earth was she thinking about? Saying something so personal to a man who was a complete stranger and had only offered her a lift out of pity?

She closed her hand over the handle, pushing the door open now, swinging her legs round heavily. The rain had lessened, so that was good at least.

'Thank you very much for the lift. It was very kind of you,' she said politely, getting out.

'You're welcome,' he replied, almost absently.

She allowed herself a glance back at him. After all, it would be the last time in her life she would ever set eyes on him. Although a man like that— from another world!—might well crop up in her dreams, or her silly mooning fantasies as she did the housework.

He was looking at her, a frown between his dark arched brows, eyes narrowed in thought, mouth set.

Just looking at her.

Looking her over.

Although she deplored it, she felt her cheeks flush, and hoped desperately he could not see. There was no reason for the flush, because his looking over was doing nothing except imprinting upon him all her un-loveliness. Frumpy, dumpy, and undeniably carrying too much weight for her height these days.

She gave an inner sigh and shut the passenger door with a slam, pausing only to raise her hand in a ten-tative wave of thanks as the car moved off down the lane leading out of the village. She gave another sigh, deeper this time, as she opened the garden gate. She had just seen the last of the most incredible-looking man she had ever seen in all her life.

Quite obviously, she would never see him again.

Except in that she was to be quite wrong...

* * *

Dante was driving again the following day, but this time far more slowly—as if he doubted whether he should be heading to this destination at all. He felt his thoughts pierce like arrows, As if he was, in fact, being entirely insane in heading there at all. Entirely insane to have in mind what he had been thinking about all night long.

But he was heading there, all the same.

When he arrived it was already late morning, and the little row of three chocolate box cottages looked ridiculously pretty in the bright early-summer sunshine, with their white picket fences and front gardens full of flowers. His eyes went to the one where he had dropped off his unintended passenger last night.

No wonder she does not wish to leave it.

He felt his thoughts churn again and silenced them. This was no time for emotion—only for cold, rational practicality. Needs must, and there would be an end to it. Rafaello had confirmed as much. Even though Raf would think Dante totally insane right now.

Dante's expression tightened even more and his mouth twisted. Well, he *was* insane—of course he was. But there was no help for it. Time, he thought as his face darkened, was of the essence. There was none to waste. He had to get this sorted—and fast.

He drew the hire car up outside the end cottage. He could see an olde-worlde pub nearby, some more pretty cottages, the medieval church and a small village shop—all very pretty, all very quaint, all very quintessentially rural England. He could see how attractive it would be to holidaymakers—and how attractive letting their cottages to them would be to their owners. There was good money to be made in high season.

Trouble was, that left no room for permanent residents...

There was no one about as he got out of the car. Deliberately, he took a deep breath, impelling himself forward lest he bottle it and cut and run instead. He swung open the garden gate and in two short strides was standing in front of a pale green door around which a climbing rose was trailing.

Lifting his hand, his face grimly set, he rapped sharply with the knocker.

Time to put his fortune to the test.

However insanely he was behaving.

CHAPTER TWO

CONNIE WAS SETTLING her grandmother in a chair in the garden. Moving her from one place to another was a slow business. Gran could not be hurried these days. She wanted things just so, and queried them several times. Connie was learning patience, showing no sign that what Gran had just asked she had already asked twice before.

That was dementia for you. Cruel, progressive, and—her heart squeezed painfully—eventually lethal.

Gran's GP had been sympathetic, but honest as well.

'Unless something else carries her off first, you must be prepared for the long haul. It could well take years—are you prepared for that?'

Yes, she was prepared. Nothing else was even to be considered. She would never willingly put Gran into a home—never!

She felt the familiar mingling of fear and dread twist in her now, as she went back indoors. The bright, cheerful smile she'd put on for Gran, who had no idea what the future was about to inflict upon her, disappeared, to be replaced by her customary expression of worry and stress.

In the little kitchen, she flicked on the kettle to make tea for them both. Then gave a start.

Someone was knocking on the door. She frowned, wondering who it could be. The rap came again, sounding impatient, and she walked warily out to the little front hall, opened the door.

As she did so, she stepped back—and saw who was standing there. Her jaw dropped and she froze on the spot.

Dante's expression did not change. But it took a degree of effort not to let it do so. *Por Dio*, he was definitely insane. He could not possibly be thinking of going through with what he'd intended.

All his angry, frustrated cogitation during the previous sleepless night had brought him to this point—but now, dear God, it was impossible...just impossible.

With an effort, he steeled himself. He was here now—no point bolting.

He nodded at the figure standing there in the doorway, staring at him open-mouthed. 'I hope you will excuse this intrusion,' he began, making his voice smooth, however rough he felt inside, 'but there is something I would like to discuss with you...if you will permit?'

For a moment her expression did not change either. It looked totally blank. Then, with a little shake, she spoke.

'What on earth is it?'

There was complete bewilderment in her voice—and something more than that, Dante detected, wondering at it.

Disbelief.

Yes, well, he thought savagely, *you and me both.*

'That, I will explain,' he answered her now, 'But not,' he added pointedly, 'on the doorstep.'

She stood back, as if yielding to his will without realising she was doing so. Maybe, he thought morosely, that was a good sign.

'Er...yes,' she said, and he saw her swallow. 'You had better come in.'

She stood aside and he walked into the tiny entrance hall, his height dominating it. A narrow staircase led upstairs, and to the right he could see a front sitting room, and to the left a kitchen. Past the stairs a corridor led to a door that stood ajar, open to the rear garden beyond. He cast a querying look at her, to indicate she should show him the way.

She did—into the kitchen.

'I just have to make a cup of tea for my grandmother. She's sitting in the garden.'

She turned away, busying herself at the kettle and with the tea caddy.

Dante took the opportunity to let his eyes rest on her. Protest rose in him. Yes, he was insane. Completely insane. Of course he could not do what he'd thought he could. He should leave—immediately.

He steeled himself again. No, he'd tough this out. He had to.

He watched as she made a mug of tea, putting in milk and a heaped teaspoon of sugar, then she cast him an apologetic glance and muttered, 'I'll just take this out to Gran.'

She walked off down the corridor to the garden door. Dante followed her. He wanted to see her grandmother. After all, this entire mad scheme rested on the elderly woman and what he'd been told last night.

As he stepped through the door he found himself on a small paved patio beyond which was a lawn, neatly mowed, bordered by flowerbeds and terminating in an area which, he could see, was a dedicated vegetable garden. A few ornamental trees marched down the edges, under one of which an ironwork bench was positioned. Like the front of the cottage, it was all ridiculously pretty.

Again, the thought came to his mind—*no wonder she does not wish to leave here.*

Then his eyes went to the occupant of a comfortable-looking wicker garden chair, old-fashioned, padded with cushions.

'Good morning,' he said pleasantly.

Blue eyes were turned slowly upon him, and in them he saw—and recognised—a vacancy that betokened the nature of her affliction. Her granddaughter was setting down the cup of tea on a table beside her, from the centre of which a parasol cast shade over the old lady's face.

'We've got a visitor, Gran. Isn't that nice?'

The voice was bright and pleasant, and designed to be cheering and reassuring.

The elderly lady said nothing, only turned her head, carefully picking up the mug of tea and taking a sip. Her gaze went back out over the garden and she seemed to relax a little. She looked calm, and peaceful too—contented, even. For a moment Dante just looked at her, a veiled expression on his face.

'You had better come inside.'

The woman he had come to see had spoken and was gesturing back into the cottage. Dante strode through the door, back to the entrance hall.

'The sitting room's probably the best place,' she suggested quietly.

He walked in and glanced around. Like the whole cottage it was small, but cosy-looking, with a chintz-covered sofa and armchair, a small open fireplace, a TV in the corner and a worn carpet on the floor.

He sat himself down on the sofa. The armchair was obviously the grandmother's, so he avoided it. The granddaughter was standing, hovering, clearly still bewildered.

Dante sat back, crossed one long leg over the other, and began. He would take charge of this affair from the start.

'You will no doubt be wondering what I have to say to you,' he opened. 'It is this. I have a proposition to put to you—a business proposition, shall we say? It will be of mutual benefit to us both. And…' He paused, then said significantly, 'And most of all to your grandmother.'

'My grandmother?'

The waitress from last night stared at him.

'Yes,' he said. 'Hear me out.'

He saw her swallow again, her hand clutching at the open door as if for reassurance. Dante's gaze took her in. She was in a pair of dark leggings, bagging at the knees, over which she wore a large, loose and completely shapeless top which did nothing for her. Its short sleeves were tight around her upper arms. Her dark hair was screwed up into a flattened knot, unflattering to her face.

A flicker of pity went through him. There were many reasons, he knew, why females neglected their appearance or turned to food for comfort, and surely, he allowed, a young woman—in her mid-twenties, he estimated—whose days were spent looking after an elderly woman with deepening dementia, had reason to find comfort where she could.

Especially if she is facing losing her home....

He saw something change in her face as he glanced at her, and immediately shuttered his gaze. It was obvious what her expression had indicated. She did not like being looked at that way and she was all too used to it.

He felt a swell of pity go through him again. Then he put the emotion aside.

Time to get down to business.

And quite definitely time to steel himself.

Connie stood there, half hanging on to the door, while the man who might as well have landed from another planet—*the planet of beautiful people*, she thought, bemused—or, indeed, stepped through from a movie screen, proceeded to set out for her what it seemed he had come to tell her.

And as he did so she felt herself wonder if there was something wrong with her ears. Because what he was saying to her was just....

Impossible.

Insane.

Absurd.

Ludicrous.

Unbelievable.

Unreal.

He fell silent finally. She stared at him, unable to speak. Unable to credit what she had heard him say. Yet say it he had.

'Well?' he prompted.

His face was without expression, and she couldn't understand why.

'You can't *possibly* be serious,' she said faintly.

Something shifted in his eyes—eyes that were quite impossible for her to look at, so she kept shearing her own gaze away. It told her that he, too, was of that opinion. And yet he had said it quite seriously. She felt an unpleasant lump form in her insides.

'It makes sense,' came the answer.

The accented voice, just as much to die for as the entire man, was cool. Impersonal.

Connie opened her mouth, then closed it. No, it did not make sense. At all.

But he was speaking again. in a calm, even tone—as if, she realised, he was forcing himself to speak.

Well, of course he is! She felt hysteria start to gather in her throat and knew why. *Of course he's forcing himself! He'd be forcing himself if he said what he's just said to any woman on earth—let alone to a woman like you.*

As she so often did, she felt colour start to rush into her face and had to fight it back. How she hated the way she looked these days—just *hated* it.

And in the presence of a man like this...

She steered her mind away. It was pointless thinking it, feeling it, giving it the slightest mental time at all. And pointless giving *him* the slightest mental time, let alone what he'd just said to her.

He was getting to his feet. He was tall—easily six feet—and the low beams which ran throughout the cottage were perilously close to the top of his head.

'I will leave you to consider what I have said,' he was saying now, and his glance at her was equally as cool and impersonal as his voice.

He was reaching into his jacket pocket and Connie could see the pale grey silk lining. The beautifully styled jacket perfectly fitted his lean, elegant form, just as his dinner jacket the night before had. He flicked out a business card, held it out to her between two fingers.

'I advise you to check out my details—that would only be prudent in the circumstances. And then please give what I have said your due consideration.'

Connie took, perforce, the business card he was still holding out.

'But I cannot give you much time. I will need a decision by the end of the week.'

She opened her mouth to speak. She could give him her decision right now—probably already had, with her stupefied reaction to his suggestion. But he did not let her.

'No.' There was the very faintest hint of a smile at the corners of his sculpted mouth. 'You must think it over. Especially as I have had more time to do so,' he pointed out.

She stared at him. 'You only met me last night—if you can even call it a meeting!' she protested.

He gave a shrug. 'I have told you. Time is of the essence. If we're going to make a deal, it needs to happen soon.'

He walked towards her, clearly intent on leaving. She stumbled backwards into the tiny hallway. He opened the front door for himself, then turned.

'It does sound insane,' he said, and now she could hear something in his voice that was almost conspiratorial, 'but there is a great deal of sanity in it.'

There was nothing she could say. Just…nothing.

Then, a moment later, there was no opportunity anyway. He had walked through the door, pulled it shut behind him, and was gone.

Connie stared. Then, turning very, very slowly, as if with no breath in her body at all, she went back into the sitting room. She stared at the sofa where he'd sat a moment ago, putting to her the most ludicrous proposal she'd ever heard in her life.

To marry a man who was a total stranger and to stay married to him for at least eighteen months... so that he could claim his inheritance and she could ensure her grandmother saw out her days in their cottage...

'I'm dreaming,' she said to herself.

It was the only explanation that made sense.

Because absolutely nothing else did...

'Raf? Answer the phone! I don't care if you're asleep, or who you're with, or if you're hung over! I need to speak to you.'

There was a pause—a long one—and Dante drummed his fingers with severe impatience on the dashboard of his car, parked outside the hotel he'd just checked out of.

He needed to get going—back to Milan. See his grandfather's lawyers, the will's executors. Tell them he was meeting his grandfather's outrageous, high-handed, damnable condition and would, therefore, be claiming his inheritance. Without further delay.

'Dante—what the hell? Where are you?'

'About to leave for London. Then Milan,' Dante's grip on his phone tightened. 'I've found her,' he said. 'The woman I can marry.'

Silence—complete silence.

Then: 'Who?' The single question came in Rafaello's best lawyer voice.

Dante took a breath. 'That waitress. The one who dropped the glasses.'

A silence even longer than the last one travelled across the ether.

Then: 'Are…you…mad?'

Three words that summed up the situation completely. Dante knew it and did not care. Could not afford to care.

'Listen,' he said. 'I'll explain.'

When he'd finished, Rafaello said frostily, 'I wash my hands of you, old friend. Until you get your sanity back.'

The line went dead.

Dante tossed his phone on to the empty passenger seat. He didn't care. He just did not care.

Face set, he gunned the engine and drove off in a roar.

A stray line from Shakespeare sounded in his head: *He must needs go that the devil drives…*

Well, the devil was driving him, all right. And he had his grandfather's face…

Connie lay staring at the low, beamed ceiling of her little bedroom. It had been her bedroom since she was eight years old, when the safe, happy world of her childhood, with parents who'd adored her and each other, had ended in a hideous car crash which had killed them both and put her in hospital for weeks.

It had been her grandmother who'd remade the world for her, bringing her to live here at the cottage, to recuperate slowly, physically and emotionally. She had stood by Connie ever since—and no way was Connie not going to stand by her grandmother now, when she needed her the most.

Getting the diagnosis of dementia nearly two years ago—when it had already been taking its toll—had been bad. Receiving the eviction notice was even worse.

Outside she could hear an owl hooting, a familiar sound, and the soft rustle of leaves, the church clock tolling the quarter hours and then the hours.

Her head was full—how could it not be? Full with so much going round and round in her head.

While her grandmother had dozed in the garden Connie had fetched her laptop, then stared at the business card of the man who had, without doubt, offered her the most bizarre proposition that could ever be imagined.

Dante Cavelli. That was his name. He'd told her that, and it was there on the stiff, expensive-looking card. *Dante Cavelli, Cavelli Finance*—that was what it said. And in Italian on the reverse side.

Carefully, she'd typed 'Cavelli Finance' into a search engine. A lot had come back, mostly in Italian, and she'd hit 'translate'. As she'd read, she'd had to admit it all seemed real—not made up, nor a scam or whatever.

Some of the links had been to articles in Italian newspapers, the economics section. And some, though far fewer, had been links to social pages. Those had come with photos.

She'd stared, taking in just how incredible-looking Dante Cavelli was. She had swallowed.

Impossible...just impossible...

A few of the photos had showed him with a grim-faced elderly man—Arturo Cavelli, founder of Cavelli Finance. More of the photos, though—and Connie had only been able to stare at them hope-lessly—had been of Dante Cavelli with a beautiful female draped over him...a wide variety of beauti-ful females...

As she'd stared, what he'd said to her had just made no sense. If he really wanted to do what he'd so un-believably said that he did—make some kind of *pro forma* marriage in order to secure his inheritance—then why on *earth* did he not just take his pick from all those women hanging on him in these photos? Chic, elegant, fashionable, beautiful...

She felt the colour run up her cheeks, mortifying and humiliating. She might almost think that what he'd said to her had been some kind of sick joke. But to what purpose?

No, he'd been serious, all right. His voice, as he'd explained, had been taut and grim. For obvious rea-sons, given what he was saying to her.

'I don't care to marry someone of my acquain-tance—she would be unlikely to understand or ap-preciate the specific limitations I am setting upon the marriage I intend to make.'

Connie had stared at the photos of all those slender, eager beauties clinging to Dante Cavelli's tall, lean, drop-dead gorgeous form, their varnished nails curving possessively around his sleeve. No, no woman in her right mind would want *any* limitations on her marrying him…

Which was why…

Which is why there is a kind of weird logic in his thinking that a female like me is preferable. Because I would never, ever get any ideas whatsoever that he might want more than he'd stated.

And what Dante Cavelli stated was very straightforward. He wanted a wife in name only, who had absolutely nothing to do with his life other than the barest minimum, ideally living in another country. They would stay married for at least eighteen months, after which a clean break divorce with a pre-agreed settlement—he'd named a sum which had made her eyes widen—would terminate their association.

But it had not been that sum which had made her breath catch; it had been something far more immediate. Far more precious to her.

'On the day of our marriage you will receive the deeds to this cottage—I will ensure its purchase… you may leave that to me—and for the duration of the marriage you will receive the monthly sum of six thousand pounds. In the event of your grandmother requiring medical treatment, or end-of-life care, this will be paid for privately, by me. I will provide a car for you, and travelling expenses, and I will also pay for a professional carer or nurse for those times when you will be required to be in my company for short periods, in order to comply with the legalities of the marriage.'

He'd gone on, and there had been a twist in his voice as he'd spoken.

'In exchange I, simply by being married, will inherit all that my grandfather has conditionally left me. I suggest that you ascertain for yourself, via the financial press, just what that entails,' he had added, his voice dry.

Well, she had checked out the financial press, and it had spelt out in black and white how very large an enterprise Cavelli Finance was, and just how very profitable it was. And how excruciatingly rich Dante Cavelli would become.

Just by getting married.

Married—as he had said that morning, sitting on her grandmother's sofa, in her grandmother's home, his tone impersonal, his expression impassive, his voice brisk and businesslike—to *her...*

She stared up at the ceiling. She could feel her heart starting to pound.

Could I do it? Could I really do it?

Oh, she might be the most unlikely woman on earth that a man like Dante Cavelli would ever marry, but so what? All that mattered were those magic words he'd said to her.

'You will receive the deeds to this cottage...'

She felt emotion strike through her—the most wonderful emotion in the world. Relief...sheer relief.

She felt tears prick her eyes. Tears of abject gratitude. Yes, of course what Dante Cavelli had proposed was bonkers—but she didn't care. Not when it would give her what she had longed for with all her being: security for her grandmother in her fading final years. That was worth anything—anything at all! Even a marriage so bizarre that no one could ever have believed it.

I'm doing it for you, Gran—all for you.

And for the first time since she had heard that a new owner had acquired the little row of cottages, and what that change of ownership would portend for her, she slept a sound and peaceful sleep. All anxiety, worry and fear vanished.

Dante stood in the waiting room at the county register office, his tension mounting. He'd sent a car to collect the woman he was about to enter into legal marriage with and it should have delivered her here by now. He'd allowed plenty of time, and yet she still wasn't here.

A dark thought possessed him. Was she going to cry off?

It was unlikely.

He glanced at the briefcase on the chair beside him. As well as the documents necessary for him to marry in the UK, it contained the deeds to the cottage—he'd bought it simply by offering the new owner a ludicrous sum for it. His hand had been all but bitten off. Just as his bride-to-be had all but bitten his hand off at his proposal.

His expression changed. But of course she had—had he expected anything else?

If you offer people what they want, they say yes.

There was the sound of someone arriving and he

turned his head to the door. His bride-to-be—arriving to get what she wanted.

Just as I am getting what I want.

His rightful inheritance.

Resentment spiked in him again. To have to go to such lengths as he was doing now in order to get that rightful inheritance was galling indeed. Marrying a complete stranger…

His eyes rested on her, studiedly impassive, as she hurriedly walked in. He should be used to her by now. They'd met, of necessity, a few times now, though each time only briefly. Once for him to receive her highly predictable answer on his return from Milan the week after he'd first put his proposition to her, and thereafter so he could brief her more fully as to how their marriage was going to play out. Then there had been the question of the pre-wedding paperwork, from birth certificates and passports to her signing the essential prenup which set out what she would get financially in their divorce.

He'd been generous, given that she was key to claiming his inheritance, but obviously he'd had to carefully limit what she could claim, given the extent of his wealth. As to his actually claiming that inheritance— immediately after the wedding they were flying to Italy, to meet with his grandfather's lawyers, to prove his married status and present his bride to them.

What they would make of her he couldn't care less— so long as they accepted that he'd met the terms of his grandfather's pernicious and damnable will, and at last released his grandfather's funds to him, so he could finally take control of all his business affairs.

'I'm sorry I'm late!' she announced breathlessly.

It was obvious she'd run up the stairs, as her colour was high, her breathing laboured. She was wearing a dress, though it was as tentlike as all her clothes—designed, it was obvious, to conceal her figure, not reveal it.

A passing thought struck Dante that of all the women he knew she was alone in not constantly demanding his admiration of her looks. Connie was the complete opposite. If anything, he'd sensed she didn't like him looking at her, so he tried not to make her self-conscious, always ignoring her less than chic appearance. Even so, he found himself noticing how the blue of her dress was bringing out the blue of her eyes. A surprisingly deep blue…

He frowned slightly.

How might she look with a little make-up, a better hairstyle, and more fashionable clothes?

He shook the thought from him. It was not relevant to the marriage he was about to make. Or the one she was about to make. As her grandmother's carer she had more on her mind than the way she looked and he respected her for that, for her dedication to her grandmother's needs, making her grandmother her priority.

She was still addressing him with apology in her voice. 'Gran was restless. She'd picked up that I was going away and was upset. The nurse you helped me engage is very nice, but Gran doesn't like change, I'm afraid.' She swallowed and looked away. 'I got a bit upset too. In the end the nurse told me to go, as me being upset was just upsetting Gran more. I'm... I'm sorry.'

Dante felt a pang of pity for her. 'Please, there is no need to apologise,' he said. 'I am sure your grandmother will settle in a day or two,' he went on, making his tone reassuring. 'And you will be home, I promise you, within a week. Now, shall we...?'

There was, after all, no point in delaying matters. They had to go through with this, each of them for their own compelling reasons.

So let's just do it.

He felt his breath tighten in his chest, his jaw set like steel. This had to be done—he had no choice.

He nodded at the door leading through to the register office itself. He saw his bride take another breath—a deeper one. Suddenly he realised she looked terrified. His own tension dropped away and he moved to her, took her hand in his. It felt clammy, but he gave it a comforting squeeze, looking down at her reassuringly. He didn't want her to feel terrified at the prospect of marrying him—she didn't deserve that.

'It will be all right. I promise you,' he said calmly. 'This is good for both of us—for you and for me. You are doing it for your grandmother. Remember that.'

He gave another brief, reassuring smile, then dropped her hand, opening the register office door and ushering her through. Inside, the registrar and several officials, two of whom would serve as their necessary witnesses, were waiting for him.

'Ah, Mr Cavelli and Miss Weston—there you are,' the registrar greeted them warmly. 'Are you both ready to proceed?'

Dante heard his bride give a gulp, but he gave the smooth, expected answer and they took their places.

The ceremony was brief, and legally binding. His bride's voice was faint, but she made the required responses in a clear and businesslike manner. As did he.

It did not take long.

And then it was done.

He was a married man.

His inheritance was finally his.

And his bride, the new Signora Cavelli, stood at his side.

It felt completely unreal.

'Do we fly to London and then to Milan?' Connie asked in the car, as they headed for the local airport.

'No, we go direct,' Dante answered her.

She frowned. 'Oh? I didn't know you could fly from here straight to Milan.'

'You can if you fly by private jet,' came the answer.

'Oh,' she said again. And then she didn't know what else to say.

Perhaps there wasn't any reason to say anything at all. Dante had got out his phone and was busy texting, completely absorbed.

With a start, she realised she should do likewise. She texted the nurse looking after her grandmother, asking after her. A reply came shortly, telling her that her grandmother was having lunch, and seemed a little less agitated. Connie was half reassured, half not.

But I have to be reassured because this has to happen—that's all.

She put the phone away in her handbag, staring out of the window with a troubled expression on her face. An air of complete and absolute unreality possessed her. But then, it had ever since Dante Cavelli had returned, as he had said he would, a week after he had walked into the cottage with his incredible offer and she had given him her reply.

Since then, everything had felt dreamlike. Including the brief civil ceremony that had just taken place.

Had the registrar wondered at how bizarre it was… marrying two people who could not have been more unalike?

If she did it's something I'm going to have to get used to—that kind of reaction from people.

She felt her heart grow heavy. How was she going to get through this coming week, being paraded as the wife of the man sitting beside her—a man who might as well be from another planet to the one she lived on?

At least it will all be in Italian… All the comments, the disbelief, the murmurings, the shock and astonishment.

Not just that Dante Cavelli had returned to Italy with a wife. But with such a wife… So completely and utterly not like the kind of beautiful, svelte, chic, elegant wife a man like him would be expected to have.

I'm nothing like that! Nothing at all—in fact I'm the very opposite.

She felt the colour start to mount in her face again and forced it back. She had no reason to feel so abashed. So what if she wasn't the kind of woman a man like Dante Cavelli was likely to marry? It was no one else's business what she and the man beside her chose to do.

She was aware that Dante was putting away his phone and turning to her. As ever, Connie gave a silent sigh. He was looking as breathtakingly drop-dead gorgeous as ever. His grey silk-lined suit had obviously been tailor-made for him, designer-styled, and he wore it with the flair that only Italian males seemed to possess. His movie star looks, those fabulously expressive dark eyes fringed with impossible lashes and his sculpted cheekbones and chiselled jaw-line—all just compounded to make her want to gaze and gaze and gaze.

But that was something she must not do. Or at least must not be caught doing. That would just be too embarrassing—mortifying, in fact.

Though he must be totally used to females gazing at him, swooning over him...

Even women who looked as unappealing as she did.

She gave another silent sigh. She'd made an effort today, dragging on a dress for the occasion, but she had known, grimly, that trying to make herself look good by styling her hair or putting on make-up would hardly turn her into a suitable bride for a man like Dante Cavelli. So she'd left well alone, content-ing herself with looking neat and tidy. It was the best she could do—and a poor best at that, as she knew all too well.

But he didn't marry me for my looks. He married me because I'll stay out of his hair—not make any demands on him!

Nor would she, of course. All she wanted was security for her grandmother and herself—and that was what she had. The deeds to Gran's cottage were now in her own handbag, and the feeling of relief at their possession was worth anything—anything at all.

'So, how do you feel?' he asked.

His voice was friendly, and she was grateful. Friendliness was really all she could cope with from him. All she would get, obviously. She knew that perfectly well. And was glad of it.

It was the way she would treat him in return. It was the only way she would be able to deal with this whole situation. As if their vastly different looks—him so gorgeous, her so totally the opposite—were simply non-existent.

It's the only way I can manage—by ignoring it.

They were, after all, simply two people solving their own respective predicaments in a way that had absolutely nothing to do with anything personal between them.

We'll just have to get on with it—deal with it, and deal with each other, in whatever way it's easiest to do so. Honest and upfront and not making a fuss....

It was therefore in a robust fashion that she answered him now. 'Weird,' Connie said bluntly. 'You must too, surely?'

He nodded. 'We'll get used to it.' He paused. 'We won't be seeing many people in Milan. Just my grandfather's lawyers—his executors.'

She frowned, a thought striking her. 'Didn't he make you one, if you're his only grandchild?'

'No,' Dante said tersely. He paused again, then spoke. 'I suspect he thought I would try and use being an executor to evade the terms of his will.'

'You said that was impossible,' Connie said.

'Precisely,' came the tight-lipped reply.

The car was turning into the airport precinct, moving towards a security gate further along from Arrivals and Departures. The gate opened and they drove slowly through. Connie could see on the Tarmac, well away from the commercial flight area, a small jet parked up. Her sense of being in a dream increased.

It did so even more as she sat herself down in a capacious leather seat—one of only a handful on board the plane. A smiling stewardess paid her some brief attention, but the bulk of it was targeted at Dante. Connie was hardly surprised. She was the kind of person people didn't notice. Dante was exactly the opposite.

He took the seat just across the aisle from her.

'Forgive me, but I will need to work during the flight,' he said to her, fastening his seat belt, and opening his briefcase. 'With our marriage I finally have clearance to make the executive decisions about Cavelli Finance that have become pressing since my grandfather died. I will be at full stretch these coming months, and I must make a start now.'

He gave her a brief smile, and soon became immersed in his work.

The stewardess was closing the plane's door, and Connie could hear the engine starting up. She sat back, a sudden feeling of excitement filling her. To be flying at all, let alone in a private jet, was a thrill.

I haven't been abroad for ages and ages...

A student jaunt—that must have been the last time. To Corfu, to celebrate her finals being over. Her face shadowed. Holidays, travel—any kind of life for herself, really—had disappeared as her grandmother's needs had increased. She'd put her life on hold.

Well, for now—just for now—she would enjoy this adventure...

The plane was taxiing, its engine note increasing, and the pilot's voice came over the intercom, informing them that they were joining the main runway. Connie peered out of her porthole, eager for take-off. It would be so exciting to feel the powerful engine lifting them skywards.

As they got their clearance, and the jet started to accelerate, she clutched the arms of her chair.

'Are you nervous?' Dante's voice was concerned as he glanced at her.

She shook head. 'No, it's brilliant!' Her eyes were shining, expression animated.

For a second—just a second—she seemed to feel Dante's gaze still on her, as if something had surprised him, but then the whoosh that came as the plane parted company with the earth was echoed in her gasp.

'Wow, you really feel it in a small plane like this!' she exclaimed.

'You do indeed,' Dante said dryly.

He seemed unaffected by the experience, and Connie realised this was probably his usual way of travelling. It brought home to her with a jolt that, except for the chauffeured car collecting her that morning, this was the first experience she'd got of just how very wealthy he was.

Thanks to me marrying him.

It was a thought she knew she needed to stay conscious of. She might be the very last female on earth that a man like Dante Cavelli would *ever* have actually chosen to marry out of personal preference, but for all that she was doing him just as big a favour as he was doing her.

I need to remember that whenever I start to feel overwhelmed by this whole thing!

Her eyes went to him. His laptop was open and his focus was on the screen. For all her determination to ignore the disparity between them, she felt something break through that dogged resolve. Something that welled up from the depths. That swept through her like a warm, liquid tide of emotion, taking her over…

How gorgeous he is! How incredibly handsome! I could never be tired of looking at him…

She felt the little plane levelling off, reaching its cruising altitude. The stewardess was walking towards them from her jump seat near the cockpit.

She smiled, but only at Dante. 'Do please let me

know when you would like me to serve lunch, Signor Cavelli. Would you like an aperitif first?'

Dante looked up, and then immediately glanced across at Connie. 'Aperitif?' he asked.

'Um…' said Connie, feeling awkward suddenly… deflated.

That strange, elated emotion drained away abruptly. In its place, another one came. A sudden and instant dislike of the stewardess, who so obviously considered her plain and frumpy and unlovely, and therefore utterly unqualified to be travelling as a passenger with the divine Signor Cavelli.

Her chin lifted, eyes sparking defiantly. 'Champagne,' she announced. 'To celebrate.'

And there was a lot to celebrate.

Dante Cavelli was going to be very, very rich, thanks to her. And she, thanks to him, was going to keep her grandmother safe for the rest of her life.

However weird their marriage was, and however bizarre, however unreal it would seem—not just to her, but to everyone else who heard about it—it was indeed, undeniably, something to celebrate.

He gave a laugh, glancing up at the hovering stewardess. 'Champagne it is,' he said warmly.

With a murmur of assent, the stewardess glided away.

'You're right,' Dante said, looking directly at Connie. 'It is something to celebrate. We've both got what we wanted. That's certainly worth toasting.'

The soft pop of a champagne cork came from the galley area, and then the stewardess was walking back with a tray on which stood two gently fizzing glasses of champagne. She offered one to Connie, with a perfunctory smile, and then, with a much warmer smile, gave the other to Dante. She glided away again.

Dante held his glass out across the aisle. 'To getting what we want,' he said to Connie.

He clinked his glass against hers, and took a mouthful of the beading liquid, as if assessing its mousse.

Connie took a sip of hers, feeling it effervesce in her mouth. Her eyes slid across to the man she had just married and she felt again that strange, irrelevant, impossible emotion well up within her—utterly and totally out of place as it was.

To getting what we want.

Dante's words echoed in her head, and in their wake came a sudden sweeping desolation.

That would never be true for her.

Never *could* be true...

CHAPTER THREE

Eleven months later...

DANTE FROWNED. The email from Connie was brief, and all the more poignant for it.

Gran is fading—it is only a matter of time, the doctor says. It's impossible to say how long, but she is now in end-of-life care.

He phoned her immediately. He could hear the tears in her voice as she spoke. He let her talk, knowing that that was what she needed to do.

He knew her better now. Even though their marriage was as minimalist as it was, some familiarity was inevitable. Though she had not come to Italy again after that first time, he'd occasionally visited her for the weekend. He'd stayed not at the cottage, which only had two bedrooms, but at one of the holiday cottages next door. The trips had been for appearances' sake, to validate their marriage for his grandfather's lawyers, but he'd found it refreshing—

relaxing, even—to be out in the countryside, away from the high-pressure demands of city life and high finance.

Connie wasn't high pressure at all—she was the complete opposite, gentle and sweet-natured—and that was refreshing too in its own way. She was so easy to be with. Familiar and undemanding.

In the time he'd spent with her they'd got more used to each other, become easier in each other's company. They might come from different countries—different worlds—yet there were similarities that resonated. Like her, he had lost his parents when he was young, and been raised by a grandparent—in that respect they were alike, and they understood each other.

He'd fallen into the habit of phoning her on Sunday evenings, listening to her talk about her grandmother, knowing it helped her to do so—to have someone to express her concerns to—and in turn he had told her about how his week had been, about the work he was doing, his clients and their interests, the destinations he was going to on business.

Sometimes those included London, and twice she'd come to stay with him there overnight, sharing a suite with him at his favourite hotel. Again, it had been to help their marriage appear real, though she had never felt easy about being away from her grandmother, even with a nurse staying in her place. It was a devotion he had respected and admired and sympathised with as dementia had taken an increasing toll on her grandmother's life.

And now, it seemed, as she told him what the doctor had said, her dementia had been compounded by a series of mini strokes, each one more incapacitating, each one weakening her grandmother further.

It was a sad business, to be sure, and he was as comforting as he could be on the phone to Connie.

'Her life is drawing peacefully to a close—her long ordeal is nearing its end,' he said sympathetically.

As was Connie's long ordeal—though he did not say that. But in their most recent meeting, when he'd gone down to the West Country to visit her, he'd been taken aback by how exhausted she was looking.

Worn out—that was the phrase that came to mind. Though he'd provided funds for external carers and nurses, Connie had insisted that she wanted to do all the care she had the strength to do herself—and if that meant interrupted nights and endless coaxing to get her grandmother to take easily digestible food, to keep her hydrated, not to mention all the difficulties of personal physical care, she had doggedly got on with it.

Though he would not dream of saying so, Dante hoped that this final stage would not last too long. It was draining all of Connie's strength—testing her to the limit.

'I'll fly over tomorrow morning,' he promised her now.

Her answer surprised him, but he knew it made sense.

'No—Dante, please. I know it sounds ungrateful,

but…but this is the last time I shall ever have Gran to myself, and I want… I want…'

She could not finish. Her voice was choked.

Immediately Dante backed off. 'If you change your mind, just say. And if there is anything else I can do—'

'No—truly, thank you. 'Connie's voice sounded disjointed. 'Dante, I have to go—that's the district nurse arriving.'

She rang off and Dante disconnected, staring at the phone for a moment. A frown furrowed his brow.

After Connie's grandmother died—what then?

What will happen to this strange marriage I've made?

He put down the phone, staring blankly at the wall, not coming up with any answer at all.

Connie sat quietly on the bench in the churchyard— the churchyard that would soon contain her poor grandmother's remains. The plot was ready—next to the husband her grandmother had lost so many years ago, long before Connie's own parents had been so tragically killed and she'd come to live with her still-stricken widowed grandmother.

The gaping earth was like a wound, raw and ago- nising, echoing the pain in her heart. Oh, she might know with her mind that her grandmother's death had been the kindest way out of the cruel clutches of dementia, but for all that she missed her with all her heart. That ache could not be eased.

Dante was coming over for the funeral. He had

been adamant. 'It is my place to be at your side,' he'd said to her, his tone quiet but firm.

And she was so very grateful to him. Not just for the financial support he'd given her as part of their deal, but for the kindness he'd shown her. The sympathy and support. It had made her feel less…alone.

Oh, her neighbours and the vicar, all the hired carers, had been sympathetic to her plight, and helpful in practical terms, but at the end of the day they all went back to their own homes. As for her friends from school and uni…well, they were all pursuing their own lives, most of them geographically far away. Being the sole carer of an elderly grandmother with dementia was very isolating, physically and emotionally, and had cut her off from the rest of life.

With Dante, for all the strangeness of their unusual marriage, which was not really a marriage at all in any normal sense, it was different. There was a link between them—a bond. A reason for them being in each other's lives, however limited, that was in a strange way comforting and reassuring. Private and personal to them.

As the months since their wedding had passed she had become far more at ease with him when they'd met out of necessity for the validity of their marriage. She had lost much of her awkwardness with him and had found him easy to talk to about her grandmother, her fears for her, and her other daily concerns. And listening to him quietly telling her about his life in Italy had been something of an escape for her too, opening a window on a world far beyond the confines of caring for Gran. He'd become familiar…reassuring.

No one here even knew she was married. She wore no wedding ring and had not changed her name. She had explained Dante's visits, and his involvement in her life, such as it was, by saying he was a cousin of her late father, who had got in touch with her and been kind enough to offer his help and support. It was plausible enough. After all, no one would believe a man like Dante Cavelli could ever think of her in any kind of romantic light.

But what was he to her now?

She swallowed, her throat tight, and her eyes went to the empty grave again. Pain tore at her, tears welling and spilling with a raw, terrible grief. Awkwardly, she got to her feet. Dusk was gathering and the rooks in the trees around the graveyard were cawing, the sound mournful and desolate. Tomorrow was the funeral service, and now she must go back to the empty cottage, have a shower, wash her hair, make herself presentable for the next day, force herself to eat something…

Her appetite had disappeared weeks ago as her grandmother had weakened so inexorably. Instead of the comfort eating that she had resorted to previously while looking after Gran, she had gone in the opposite direction, picking at her food, pushing away her still-full plates. The pounds had dropped off her, but she couldn't care less. Her appearance had never mattered—not since she'd dedicated herself to her grandmother's care. And it certainly did not matter to Dante…

Into her head flitted what Dante had said as they had flown off after their wedding.

'To getting what we want.'

Well, that was just what they *had* got. He'd got his inheritance, and she had got security for her grandmother for the rest of her days. And now those days were over…

Tears of loss choked her again. The funeral tomorrow would be unbearable.

But I will have Dante at my side, to help me through it.

It was her only comforting thought, and she clung to it with surprising strength.

Dante stood beside Connie by the waiting grave as the pallbearers slowly lowered their burden into it and the vicar intoned the solemn words of the Committal. At his side, shoulders hunched in the concealing black coat she was wearing, Connie wept silently.

His memories went back to the funeral of his grandfather. His grief had been infused with shock— the suddenness of the fatal heart attack, unexpected, despite his grandfather's age. He had seemed so indomitable. As if he would go on for ever. Instead, he had died, leaving his grandson completely alone in the world.

As Connie is now too.

It was a strange thought…that both of them had no one else at all.

Except each other.

The thought was fleeting—disturbing. He put it aside. The Committal was ending, the vicar was intoning the final words, and a sob was audibly breaking now from Connie.

Instinctively, he put his arm around her shoulder, in an urge to give her the kind of natural human comfort she so obviously needed. He could feel the shaking of her body as she wept. It was strange to feel her so close to him—but it felt right, too. At his grandfather's funeral he had stood completely alone…no one at his side. No one with any claim on him—or he on them.

The funeral was complete. Dante's thoughts came away from his own memories to the present moment. It was time to leave the graveside, and he and the vicar guided Connie down the path across the churchyard. There would be no wake, as Connie had said she could not face it, and he understood.

They took their leave of the vicar at the lychgate and he walked her back to her cottage. Connie's head was still bowed, tears undried on her cheeks, shoulders hunched. She looked, thought Dante with concern, shrunken and lost…

Inside the cottage he guided her into the little sitting room, helped her off with her coat. The black material of her mourning dress seemed to hang on her, too loose for any semblance of elegance. But what did appearance matter at a time like this? Her expression was haunted, eyes too large in her face.

A memory pierced him out of nowhere. Of how

he'd first noticed, so incongruously, the vivid blue of her eyes on their wedding day all those long months ago. And then how they'd shone so brilliantly with excitement as the jet winging them to Milan had taken off, animating her face, lifting her features. Now they were smeared with tears, red-rimmed with weeping.

'I will make you a cup of tea,' he informed her.

It was the English remedy for all ills. Even grief...

When he came back, mug of tea in hand, and one of instant coffee for himself, she had not moved. She was sitting inertly on the sofa, gazing blindly at the armchair, empty now. Empty for ever. Memory hit him again—a different scene this time.

He lowered the mug of tea to the small table by the sofa. 'When I went into my grandfather's study the day of his funeral,' he heard his own voice say, 'I could not bear to see his chair behind his desk. To know he would never sit there again—'

He broke off. Swallowed. Death was hard. However it happened.

He sat down abruptly at the far end of the small sofa, curving his hands around his own mug. Connie turned her head, as if it weighed too much, and looked at him through her tears.

'I see her there... Gran. In her chair. Though she has not sat there for weeks...'

Her voice was low, thready, exhausted.

Dante's, as he answered her, was low as well.

'It will ease in time. I promise you,' he said. He frowned, looking away, down into his coffee. 'In the end, there will only be good memories left.'

Even as he spoke he knew that was not completely true. He had many good memories, yes—but not all were good. His sense of hurt—betrayal—at the conditions in his grandfather's will still remained like a canker. A jab of emotion came—bitter and harsh. His eyes lifted to the woman sitting there beside him. A woman he'd had to marry...who'd been a complete stranger to him.

But she was no longer a stranger...

She was once again shifting her gaze to the empty chair where her grandmother would never sit again, bleakness in her expression.

'I miss her so *much*,' she said haltingly. 'I cannot bear it that she's gone. That I will never see her again—never...'

He saw tears filling her eyes again, misting the deep blue that he'd so seldom noticed, making them grey with grief.

Pity filled him.

She was a woman who, without the machinations of his grandfather's malign will, he would never have known at all. Yet now she sat beside him, haunted in her grief, the most extreme of all emotions, calling echoes in himself.

We both lost our parents. Each only had a grandparent for so much of our lives. And now we don't have even that.

Without realising it, he slipped one hand from cupping his coffee, moved it sideways, picked up one of the hands, lying so inertly in her lap. He took it into his. Her hand felt warm and soft. The sofa was small, and she was only a short distance from him. He'd only have to draw her against him, take her into his arms, to give her the human comfort that grief allowed.

Only grief?

Was that all it was?

His gaze went to her. Her face, so tear-stained, seemed gaunt and strained, and yet there was something about it—a haunted quality that accentuated her cheekbones, sculpted her mouth, deepened those eyes brimming with more as yet unshed tears, like diamonds on her eyelashes.

For a moment he felt something within him that had never been there before…a sense of closeness he'd never experienced.

Because I am remembering my grandfather just as she is remembering her grandmother? Is that why?

He did not know. Knew only that he kept her small hand in his. He went on sitting there quietly, saying nothing. Silence all around them. Between them. Only broken by the ticking clock on the mantelpiece.

He felt her fingers tighten over his. And it seemed to him, in that moment, that it was right that they should do so.

He did not stay much longer. Though of course he had offered to stay, Connie had said she wanted to be alone, and he respected her wishes.

But as he took his leave, he turned to her by the cottage front door. 'Connie…' He paused. Then, 'If there is anything you need—anything at all—you must phone me at once and I'll be here. Do you understand? I know this is hard for you...so very hard.'

Her voice was strangled as she answered, half lifting her head to look at him. 'Thank you—it's kind—but...'

He nodded again. She was at the end of what little strength had remained to her.

He reached for her hand, squeezed it lightly, then let it go. 'You can be proud of what you did,' he said, his voice intent. 'You saw her through the last of her life to her passing beyond it. You were a loving, loyal granddaughter, and you gave her your love and loyalty to the very end.' Something changed in his voice as suddenly he knew there was something he urgently wanted her to hear. 'And now, Connie, now she is free—do you understand?'

She didn't answer him. She could not speak, he could see. And her head had bowed again, tears flowing once more. She didn't look at him—could not, he could see that too—but turned away, shoulders shaking, completely breaking down. She all but stumbled back indoors, pulling the door shut, disappearing inside.

For a moment Dante just stood there, disquieted and concerned. Then, knowing she truly did not wish him to be there, he took a breath and walked away, lowering himself into his car, and driving off.

Heading back to his own, quite separate life. The way he wanted it to be.

* * *

Connie lay on her bed, all alone in the cottage.

I'm on my own now...completely on my own.

Except for—

No, that was not something to be thought. She must not think of Dante in that way. She had no claim on him. No real claim...

I mustn't think anything otherwise. I just mustn't— however kind he is, and however much he supported me over Gran's death and funeral.

Thoughts moved in her head, difficult and painful. The sense of loss still overwhelmed her, but with part of her mind she was also aware that with her grandmother's death her life had changed for ever.

Or had it?

Dante had made it clear that he wanted their marriage to last at least eighteen months—which was still seven months ahead. So, were they supposed to continue as they had been doing while her grandmother was alive? She didn't know, and right now she could not focus on it. Dante was back in Milan and she was here, in the cottage she called home, filled still with the presence of the grandmother she had loved so much.

For now, it was all she could cope with. All she could cling to with her grieving heart.

Dante opened the email from Connie, reading what he'd expected to read. Her grandmother's probate had gone through as smoothly as he'd assured her it would—he'd asked Rafaello to glance over the brief will, but Connie's grandmother had had little to leave her granddaughter after the cost of her care.

His expression shadowed. It had been Rafaello who'd put to him the question that Dante felt take shape again in his mind now, as he read Connie's email.

'What's going to happen now, Dante?' he'd asked. 'You made this marriage on the assumption that Connie would likely be looking after her grandmother for the duration. Would therefore always need to be based in England. But now...?'

Dante had batted his friend's concern away.

'Let the poor girl be, Raf! She's only just buried her grandmother. Time enough for future plans. I don't want her hassled or upset even more.'

Had he sounded defensive? Protective, even? Well, if he had, he wasn't sorry for it.

Raf had stared at him, a quizzical look in his eye. Dante hadn't liked it. Raf had had that damn perceptive lawyer's expression on his face, as if he was all too eager to probe beneath the surface of Dante's response.

Well, there was nothing *to* probe! Though Raf had made his objections to his impulsive and desperate marriage clear enough, once it had been done, he'd kept quiet about it. He'd met Connie briefly, when she'd come to Italy to be presented to Dante's grandfather's lawyers, and been perfectly civil to her, if somewhat guarded. As for himself, whenever he'd met up with Raf, or chatted with him online, he'd never *not* mentioned Connie, or the contact he had with her. He'd been completely open about her. Why shouldn't he be?

'Will she come out to Milan now?'

Raf had followed the quizzical look with that direct question. A question Dante hadn't wanted to hear, let alone answer.

'Why should she?' he'd countered.

The quizzical look had changed into something different, less easy to interpret. It had annoyed Dante even more.

'Raf, apart from my grandfather's lawyers, you're the only person who knows about Connie...knows that I'm married. And I want to keep it that way. There's no reason not to. Connie's a lovely girl and I've got used to her...to the fact she's in my life for the reasons she is. I'm fond of her, even. She's been through a lot, and I'm glad I've been of help to her, that she had me to turn to. But—'

He'd broken off, still not liking Raf's expression. Anyway, Connie and his relationship with her, such as it was, was none of Raf's business! It wasn't anyone's business but his and Connie's.

He'd drawn a sharp breath and said, *'Our marriage still has more than six months to run—Raf, you told me yourself that was the minimum length to fulfil the terms of that benighted will! As to how those months are going to pan out now... Well, I'll work something out with Connie.'*

Yes, but what? He hadn't come up with an answer for Raf, and he hadn't come up with an answer for himself either. But something had to be done—that was the thing.

His brows drew together in a frown. So what would Connie do now? What *should* she do? They'd been able to live almost completely separate lives from each other, just as he'd intended from the off, because her circumstances had been such that she'd had good reason to live in a different country from him. But now that reason was gone.

Raf's question rang in his ears again.

'What's going to happen now?'

He was still not getting an answer.

Connie stared at herself in the mirror set into the old-fashioned wardrobe in her grandmother's bedroom, hating the way she looked.

It was a familiar feeling. Had been for a long time.

When she'd been a student she'd thought she looked OK, even though she'd always had the kind of figure that could end up a little plump if she wasn't careful, but when she'd had to start looking after Gran her social life had disappeared, and she'd had neither the time, nor the inclination, nor any purpose in caring what she looked like. It just hadn't seemed important.

And also, she thought depressingly, the more she'd let herself go, the worse it had got. Once she'd piled on the pounds with her comfort eating, it had seemed pointless to pay any attention to her hair, or her complexion, let alone to what she wore. It had all gone swiftly downhill from there.

She gave a defeated sigh. The irony now was that in the stress of the final weeks of her grandmother's life she'd totally lost her appetite, and she'd shed most of those extra pounds. But she was still untoned and unfit...

She turned away, not wanting to look at herself a moment longer, reaching for a baggy tee shirt to pull over her bra and pants and hoisting herself into a pair of loose cotton trousers. Camouflage clothing. She had a lot to camouflage.

That sense of depression washed over her. Looking after her grandmother had been her life—but now Gran was gone. So what came now? She knew she must make an effort, must not let herself sink any deeper, but it was so hard to find any sense of purpose right now. She tried to think back to what her hopes and dreams had been before she'd set them aside to devote herself to Gran. She'd been undecided, she remembered, torn between continuing her studies, getting her Master's, or starting a career—maybe in publishing...something like that? Or perhaps she'd just take off...go travelling for a while before settling down?

The trouble was it all seemed so daunting now—and it was impossible to focus her mind on anything at all, as fuzzy as it was. Everything seemed like a major effort...just getting all the paperwork after a death completed had been hard for her.

She stomped downstairs, closing in on herself. What would Gran want for her? She paused as she went into the living room, ready to pass the time dully watching TV programmes she paid no attention to. She caught a glimpse of herself in the mirror over the fireplace. Her hair was pulled back off her face, as it always was, plain and unlovely.

You should get your hair done, Connie, dear.

She stilled. It was almost as if she could hear her Gran's familiar voice from long ago, before dementia had gripped her so tightly.

You've let yourself go—and that's such a shame. It's time you spoilt yourself a little!

It came again—and though she knew she was imagining it Connie felt a trickle of warmth go through her. Had dementia not clouded Gran's mind she would have deplored the way Connie had given up on herself. She felt herself take a breath—a deep one.

Maybe that was what she should do. Not try to think too far ahead but focus instead on something more immediate. Something to make her feel better both in herself and for herself. Stop letting herself go—start getting herself back again.

It could be done…

But I don't want it to take for ever. I don't want to do it little by little, or I'll slip back into bad old ways. It would be all too easy to go back to comfort eating—especially here, with so much pulling me down, missing Gran so much. I want something to stop me backsliding…to make me keep at it intensively, productively. Something like a boot camp or a health spa, maybe?

Almost without realising it, she picked up her laptop, plonking herself down on the sofa. Could she really do this? Places where they licked you into shape did not come cheap…

But I've spent almost nothing of all that money Dante kept paying into my account—there's pots and pots of it, just sitting there!

She clicked on to the Internet, keying in her search terms. For the first time in a long time the blanketing fog of grief and depression seemed to lift as she searched for what she needed…

Dante was reading another email from Connie—a surprising one this time. It was telling him she was heading to the Lake District, of all places. She'd booked herself into a wellness resort. For a month.

He read it again, as if to convince himself it was actually what she'd said. The very idea was totally unlike the Connie he knew. She was a home girl… unhappy if she was away from her beloved cottage.

But that was when she was looking after her grandmother.

Now that was no longer a necessity.

Yet the thought of Connie at a health spa, let alone one hundreds of miles from where she lived, was still a startling one.

On the other hand, he mused, maybe it would do her good. She could do with some pampering, thinking about herself for a change, not her grandmother's needs. Yet he was conscious of having mixed feelings. He would not need to worry about her while she was there. Nor spend any time thinking about her for a while…thinking about what she was going to do with her life now that her grandmother was no more.

With a slight feeling of discomfort he realised that, if he were to be completely honest, he would have preferred it if Connie's grandmother had *not* died when she had. Not just for Connie's sake—but for his own. While Connie had been nursing her grandmother, he'd known where he was with her. But now…?

Now it was much more complicated.

Selfishly, he acknowledged ruefully, his preference would be for Connie simply to go on living as she had, in her cottage, until it was OK for them to get divorced. But that, he knew, was a completely self-centred preference. What if Connie didn't want to go on living as she had? Wanted something new in her life?

But what could that be?

And, whatever it was that she wanted, how would it impact him?

He just did not know—and he didn't like that feeling.

Connie felt the treadmill slow into cool-down mode and satisfaction filled her. Ten kilometres at a modest but definite incline. And though her heart rate was elevated, she wasn't puffing and breathless. A distinct change from when she'd first arrived at the spa.

And it wasn't just her physical fitness either.

The complete change of scene and daily activity had transformed her. Opened the lid of the box of grief and bereavement she'd been closing herself into.

Up here in the Lake District, with the lakes and the peaks, the dramatic beauty of the stark, wild landscape, she'd felt her spirits lift imperceptibly day by day. And as for the wellness resort…

She gave a wry smile now as she stepped off the treadmill and headed towards the fixed weights section of the superbly equipped workout area. She would never, *ever* have thought she'd actually enjoy the vigorous facilities it offered, and yet it was filling her with satisfaction and a wonderful sense of achievement that she had put herself in the hands of the skilled personal trainer who oversaw her exercise regime. He had drawn up a programme that put her long-neglected body through its paces, toning and trimming, stretching and sleeking, day by day turning flab into fit…

Nor had she confined herself to the gym, either. The resort came with an indoor training pool, there was aquarobics, yoga and Pilates sessions, as well as all the sybaritic pampering treatments she'd so self-indulgently splashed out on—because, after all, she might as well, while she was here, and daily massages felt well deserved after all her exertions in the gym. But most restoring of all to her spirits, she knew, was access to plentiful mountain and lakeside walks that let her get out into the fresh air, breathe deeply, and achieve, little by little, day by day, a new perspective on life.

It was impossible not to feel the fog of grief lifting, as, her workout completed, a light but nutritious and healthy lunch consumed, she headed off outdoors each day into the bright, bracing air, to gaze at the grandeur all around her as she strode up the fell towering over the deep, dark lake.

Impossible not to start to want to re-join the world she had withdrawn from for far too long.

Impossible not to accept that embracing life again was what her grandmother would want for her.

In her head she could hear Gran's voice, warm and loving.

Go out and live, my dearest, dearest girl, for my sake—and for yours.

She felt Gran's blessing on her every day—including this one.

Felt, too, more unwelcome thoughts plucking at her. And although this was harder, she knew she would have to face up to it when the time came, as soon it must.

Face up to letting Dante leave my life. Going our separate ways.

She knew it must be so—and yet a pang of grief of a different sort pierced her. From the very start their marriage had been only a means to an end, for both of them, but as the weeks and months had passed, even with the limited contact they'd had with each other, she knew that Dante had become…

Important to me.

She paused by her usual viewpoint on the fell as she gained elevation, her expression troubled suddenly. Forbidden thoughts came to her as words returned once again to her mind. The toast Dante had made on the plane that day so many months ago.

'To getting what we want.'

Something clutched at her insides. She had known then that what she wanted was so much more than he did.

Because what she wanted—dreamt of—yearned for—was impossible.

Surely it was.

Wasn't it?

Dante closed down his laptop and slid it into his monogrammed leather briefcase, then checked his seat belt as the plane started its descent into Heathrow. He was fitting in a trip to the UK because Connie had finished her stay at the wellness resort she'd taken herself off to, and he really did need to talk to her about what was uppermost in his mind. And hers too, no doubt.

With her caring duties ended sooner than either he or Connie had anticipated, what did she plan to do with her life?

Until it's possible for us to get on with our divorce.

The divorce that would finally set him free from his grandfather's control.

Why did he do it to me? I did everything he ever wanted of me and still he betrayed me...

The old painful question rose again in his head, and he pushed it away. There was no point letting it in. He'd found a way to cope with the hurt, and he had to try and move on. His expression changed, became rueful. The conditions of his inheritance might have been malign, but that had never been a term to apply to the woman who had made it possible for him to fulfil them!

A half-smile played around his mouth and he felt his tension ease. He'd lucked out with Connie, that was for sure. Oh, it was not just that she was the perfect wife for his highly imperfect circumstances, needing to live a thousand miles away from him to look after her ailing grandmother, but because…

He paused mentally. Because what, precisely?

Because she's a sweet, kind person, and in my own way I've grown fond of her.

Of course he didn't actually see her as a wife—not a real one. He didn't see any female as a wife and settling down with anyone wasn't on his agenda. He wanted freedom, untrammelled by anyone making claims on him, whether that was his grandfather, or any woman his grandfather wanted to saddle him with.

Or Connie.

His thoughts returned full circle. How were they going to see out the remaining few months of their marriage? His thoughts went back to casual conversations, snippets and bits and pieces they'd chanced to have in the times they'd met up or chatted on the phone, or things said in emails. She'd mentioned, hadn't she, that after graduating she'd been torn between staying on to get her Master's, or getting stuck into building a career, maybe in publishing, or something in that sort of world? Then, of course, all that had been derailed by her grandmother's worsening health, and Connie had put all her plans and ambitions on hold.

But now Connie was free to take them up again. To do something with her life that was her own.

Whatever it is she wants to do I'll support her—of course I will.

And of course she'd want to stay in England, wouldn't she? Whether it was to continue with academic life or get a job. That would suit him perfectly.

I can rent an apartment for her, wherever she wants to be based. And I can go on dropping in on her, or we can meet up in London—whatever is necessary to make our marriage still look genuine.

Besides, he mused, if she was working in the UK, or continuing her studies, that would be reason enough why she was not living with him in Italy. His grandfather's lawyers surely couldn't kick up about that, could they? Since she'd had to put her own life on hold to nurse her grandmother, it would be natural that she'd want to pick up her career or her studies now she was free to do so.

He settled back into his airline seat as the plane came into land, his mood definitely improved. He'd have tonight in London, then head to the West Country tomorrow. From Connie's texts and emails, it seemed she'd enjoyed herself at the resort. It was nice to think of her pampering herself for once. Starting a new life after what she'd been through.

Just as I will—finally—once I'm free of a marriage I never wanted.

It was a cheering thought.

Wasn't it?

He shook his head impatiently. Of course he wanted to be free of his marriage. Free of its fetters and constraints.

A frown formed on his brow as the plane taxied to its stand. Free of marriage—yes, definitely. But free of Connie…? His frown deepened, then cleared. Just because they'd be divorced it didn't mean he'd cut her out of his life completely—why should it? They could go on seeing each other, meeting up from time to time, just as they did now, and having the same relaxing, easy-going relationship. Well, friendship, really, as that was what it had become. After all, why not?

He was used to her, liked her and respected her. He enjoyed her company, was even fond of her. That was enough—more than enough.

In good humour, he prepared to disembark.

Connie stepped into the taxi carefully, settling herself with care in the capacious seat.

'Where to?' the London cabbie enquired over his shoulder.

She gave the name of Dante's hotel, conscious of butterflies in her stomach. She was not surprised at their presence—not least because Dante had assumed she was going to be at home at the cottage, not here in London.

She fished out her phone, tapping out a message. His flight had landed, and she knew he always stayed at the same hotel on Piccadilly when he was in London.

Dante, hi—I've ended up coming south via London. Can I come to your hotel? Is half-six OK?

As she sent it, she wondered whether it would suit him for her to be in London tonight. Maybe he had made other plans for the evening? Well, too late now. And if she didn't go through with this tonight, she'd lose her nerve completely.

She felt the butterflies swoop inside her again, staring at the blank phone screen as the taxi made its slow way through the busy London traffic from Knightsbridge.

Was she mad to be doing what she was?

The butterflies swooped again. And then again as Dante's reply flashed up.

It conveyed surprise that she wasn't at the cottage, but made no objection to her coming to his hotel.

I'll be in the cocktail bar.

She texted back a quick thumbs-up and then sat back, letting the butterflies swoop again.

And go on swooping…

CHAPTER FOUR

DANTE GLANCED AT his watch. Nearly ten to seven. They'd agreed half-past six. Ah, well, she probably wasn't used to London traffic at this hour, slowing down the taxis. He still wasn't sure why she'd come via London at all—it was hardly en route to the West Country from the Lake District. Still, it would save him driving down to the cottage. And a couple of days in London would do Connie good, he thought.

He'd booked them in for dinner at the hotel's excellent restaurant, and changed his room to a suite. Maybe tomorrow night she'd like to go to a show, or a play? London's West End provided a rich choice. He'd ask her tonight. As well, of course, as starting the necessary conversation about what she wanted to do with her life going forward.

Another pleasing thought struck him. Now that she'd spent time pampering herself at the wellness resort, while she was in town he could encourage her to indulge herself some more—go shopping, buy some new clothes, have her hair done…that sort of thing. He'd always felt sorry for her, even though he'd understood why the last thing she'd cared about was the way she looked. But now, surely, she could focus on herself for a change.

Memory sifted through him—how he'd noticed all those months ago that, despite her baggy clothes and scraped-back hair, she had incredibly lovely eyes. Blue, deep-set, long lashed… In fact, the most beautiful he could remember seeing on a woman.

The barman placed the second martini he'd ordered in front of him, and Dante took an appreciative sip. The bar was filling up and he glanced at his watch again—more impatiently this time. Nearly seven and still no sign of her.

The pianist settled at the white baby grand in the corner really was very attractive, he thought.

He flicked his eyes away. No, not appropriate…

He moved his gaze on, resting it on the entrance to the lounge, as he took a mouthful of his martini. Then, just as he started to lower it back to the surface of the bar, he stilled. A woman had just walked into the lounge and paused, standing in the entranceway. Framed in the light.

And this time it was totally impossible for Dante to move his gaze away…

Connie paused, the butterflies inside her now starting to flap manically. It had taken more nerve than she'd thought it would just to walk into the hotel lobby. Now, though, she was going to need every bit of courage she possessed. For an abjectly cowardly moment she wished she was back at her cottage, hundreds of miles away. Not here, and about to do what she was going to do.

Her thoughts skittered. She did not want to think about why she was doing it. It had been an impulse on leaving the resort, feeling so good about herself for the first time in a long time. She'd wanted to keep that going—build on it. To head for London and meet up with Dante there, not at the cottage.

At the cottage in the country she'd just be the same old Connie. But here, meeting him at his elegant five-star hotel, where she'd always felt overly conscious of the frumpy, dumpy way she looked...

Surely that justified what she'd done today? That was why she'd done it, wasn't it? Gone shopping for the outfit she was wearing. To look more the part for a swanky hotel. Not for any other reason. None she would admit to, anyway.

Or dare admit to...

A sudden fear struck her as she walked to the entrance of the cocktail lounge. She was about to come face to face with Dante. She hadn't seen him since the funeral, weeks and weeks ago. And now, after her time at the resort, after what she'd done today in London...

Will he think me ridiculous?

Fear darted in her. Then subsided. If he did think her ridiculous...well, he would not show it. She knew him well enough to be certain of that. He'd always been courteous, tactful—*kind*, in fact, about how utterly different she was from the type of women a man like him would normally be seen with. Her self-consciousness, she knew, came from herself—not from Dante making her feel it tactlessly or cruelly.

She swallowed, still nervous, pausing in the entrance to the dimly lit cocktail lounge, unaware that she was silhouetted against the brighter light of the lobby behind her. She let her eyes adjust, heard low blues music coming from a grand piano nearby, wondering where Dante was.

Then, with relief, she saw him, and her breath caught as it always did. He was sitting on one of the tall bar stools, looking as effortlessly fabulous as usual.

He was in a business suit. The dark silk of his tie contrasted with the pristine whiteness of his shirt, and she could see the glint of his gold watch strap around the wrist of the hand holding his martini glass. His sable hair, immaculately cut, feathered over his brow and the nape of his neck. His features, as ever, looked as if he were gracing a movie screen.

She gave a familiar inner sigh.

It was exactly the same breath-stilling impact he'd made on her the very first time she'd set eyes on him at that wedding reception, unable to tear her gaze away from him.

For a second—an instant only—she felt emotion flare through her, pain and longing. Familiar and, oh, always so hopeless…

But she couldn't just stand there like a dummy, gazing upon the physical perfection that was Dante. She gave a slightly jerky lift of her hand, to indicate that she'd seen him, but he did not return it. He seemed to be quite motionless. She started forward, burningly self-conscious, heading towards him.

It was only a short distance to where Dante was sitting, still unmoving, his martini glass suspended in his hand. His face was utterly expressionless, and she felt her heart start to thud uncomfortably, nerves plucking at her, breath tight in her lungs.

She stopped dead in front of Dante, stuttering a little as she said, 'Um…sorry I'm late. The traffic was awful.'

Dante still hadn't moved. Hadn't said a word. His face frozen in that blank expression. Then…

'Connie?'

The disbelief in his voice was searing. She felt colour flush up her cheeks, and for one hideous moment she felt like the biggest fool in the world. Humiliation rushed like a furious tide in her veins.

Oh, God, he thinks me completely ridiculous!

Her face worked. She swallowed painfully. Then something broke from him in rapid Italian, which she couldn't make out.

He swapped to English, his expression still incredulous. 'You look absolutely *amazing*!'

The warmth in his voice was like a balm to her. And the expression in his eyes…

She felt heat rise in her, and a sense of wonder so deep that it made her feel faint. Her legs were suddenly weak. Everything in her was trembling. She was made weak by the way he was looking at her, the way his gold-flecked dark, expressive, long-lashed eyes were fixed on her. Warm. Appreciative. Admiring.

She grabbed at the empty bar stool next to his and hoisted herself up onto it, needing its support. Her heart rate was hectic, and there was still a strange, utterly novel and incredible feeling coursing through her.

Because Dante Cavelli is looking at me....

And looking at her as he had never looked at her before.

As I have always longed for him to look at me...

'I've had a makeover,' she said. Probably unnecessarily. She took a breath. 'It started at the resort, getting myself fit again, getting back into shape, eating sensibly, taking exercise and long walks. Then today... Well, I've spent the afternoon in Knightsbridge, having my hair done, professional make-up, all that stuff—and buying this dress.' She looked abashed for a moment. 'It was hideously expensive, Dante, but for once I just wanted to splash out!'

As she spoke she was blissfully conscious of the way his intent gaze was resting on her. She knew it was the exquisitely beautiful dress that had grabbed his attention. Slub silk, peacock-blue, it hugged her newly svelte, tautly toned body so lovingly, accentuating her enticing curves, moulding her breasts, skimming her sheer-stockinged legs. Not only that, but her newly cut, coloured and chicly styled hair, and her complexion-flattering, eye-deepening, cheekbone-enhancing make-up, including the most luscious lipstick, was all creating exactly the impression she'd hoped for, and Dante's response made her head spin.

Elation coursed through her, and she was only

dimly aware that the barman had approached them, asking her what she might like to drink. She blinked for a moment, and a sudden memory came to her of that snooty stewardess on the private jet winging them to Milan on her wedding day...of how she'd all but ignored the frumpy, dumpy, badly dressed female presuming to travel with so divine a male as Dante Cavelli.

'Champagne,' she heard herself say, just as she had said so defiantly to that disdainful stewardess. 'A champagne cocktail, please.'

As the barman nodded and glided away, she turned to Dante. There was still a look of incredulity in his expression, and it warmed her just as much as the open admiration in his eyes.

She gave a little laugh. 'I can hardly believe it myself,' she admitted. 'A posh frock and all the trimmings works wonders!'

He gave an answering laugh, warm and appreciative. 'Ah, it was there all along, Connie. But you had other, more important things to focus on.' He nodded. 'Now you can start to live your own life.'

A shaft of sadness shadowed her face. 'I wouldn't have had it any other way, Dante, truly not.' Her voice lifted, 'But all the same I know Gran would want only good things for me.'

The barman was placing her champagne cocktail in front of her, and she lifted the glass. Dante did likewise with his martini glass.

'To all the good things for you, Connie,' Dante toasted, his voice as warm as his eyes.

Into her head, yet again, came the toast he had given on the private jet on their wedding day.

'To getting what we want...'

The words hung in her mind, mingling with those he'd spoken just now. Teasing her. Tempting her...

She took a mouthful of her cocktail.

And promptly choked.

Grabbing a nearby paper napkin, she clutched it to her lips. 'Oh, my God! What's *in* that?' she exclaimed hoarsely.

A laugh broke from Dante. 'You mean apart from the maraschino cherry and the slice of orange, and the added sugar? Well, Angostura bitters for bite, and a hefty slug of cognac for punch. It's the cognac that gives it its kick,' he said kindly.

'Oh, my God,' she said again. 'I thought it would be just champagne diluted with juice. You know... orange or peach or something.'

'That's a Buck's Fizz or a Bellini,' Dante informed her. His eyes met hers, and once again the high-voltage charge of terror mixed with excitement went right through her. 'But this moment definitely calls for something with a kick.'

Something changed in his expression...something she could not read this time.

'Just as you have given me a kick I never thought was possible, Connie.'

He reached his hand out to her just lightly, touching the fall of her hair, then dropping back. Then he tapped the rim of his glass against hers again.

'Drink up.' He smiled. 'But this time just sip, OK?'

Bravely, Connie did just that. She was ready for the kick this time.

Ready for so much more…

And those butterflies soared again, iridescence in their wings.

Dante was still in something of a disbelieving daze. His incredulous eyes kept going to Connie across the table in the hotel restaurant, where they had repaired once she had cautiously finished her champagne cocktail, and he—much less cautiously, for he'd felt strongly that he needed something to deal with what was coursing through his veins—had demolished the rest of his martini.

His gaze went to Connie yet again, as though magnetised. He'd guessed that with some pampering and new clothes she might look different from the way he'd become used to, but this…

Her upswept hair, tinted a rich mahogany, was styled so that delicate tendrils whispered around her face, and her eyes, already deep and blue, with the aid of subtle make-up were now so much deeper and so much bluer that he blinked. Her mouth was accentuated with rich lipstick and her delicate cheekbones sculpted with blusher. And, of course, there was that stunning cocktail dress in shimmering shades of peacock-blue and green which skimmed lovingly over her svelte curves and was utterly perfect on her.

Oh, the whole impact was just as he had exclaimed—*amazing*. Somewhere deep inside, at the very centre of him, he felt a low, dark purr start up.

But he didn't want to over-focus on the physical impact she was having on him. He knew very well that there was more to her than that. Oh, she was still Connie as he had come to know her—natural and unpretentious and open and sweet-natured—but now… He tried to give words to his thoughts. Now, he could see a glow about her—a new confidence, a sense of vitality that she'd been missing. It was as if she were rediscovering, reclaiming, something of her own. Something that had been put aside in her years of caring for her grandmother.

She can look forward to the future now—with new confidence in herself, new assurance, new hopes and prospects.

He was glad for her—and he said as much now.

'I feel this is the beginning of something new and exciting for you, Connie,' he said. 'And you deserve it—you truly do.'

He lifted his wine glass, took an appreciative sip of the expensive vintage. He wanted Connie to have a wonderful evening, to celebrate this fresh start to her life.

'Tell me, have you any thoughts…ideas…about what might come next for you?'

For a moment he thought he saw something in her eyes—but it was gone before he could identify it.

'Well, I feel a lot fitter—thanks to all those weeks at the resort—and with more energy too.'

Her voice changed, and again Dante felt there was something in it that he could not quite place.

'I know that with Gran gone I have to look forward

now. Pick up the reins of my life again.' She frowned a little. 'I'm just not really sure quite yet what I want, or how to go about it.'

He took a forkful of his melt-in-the-mouth lamb.

'You used to tell me that you'd once considered doing a Master's degree,' he reminded her. 'Is that still a possibility? An ambition?'

'I'm not sure. Maybe I should job-hunt instead. Although…' She bit her lip. 'To be honest, lovely as the cottage is, there aren't a lot of jobs around there that require any knowledge of English literature!'

'Move here—to London,' he said promptly. 'Loads more options.'

She made a face. 'Accommodation here is fiend-ishly expensive. On the other hand,' she mused, 'that incredibly generous allowance you made me is mostly sitting in the bank still. I used a wodge of it for my month at the resort, but it would fund me for a good while here in London, until I get settled with a job and a salary.'

'I'd be happy to rent a flat for you,' Dante replied. 'After all, you are my wife!'

She shook her head decisively. 'I couldn't possibly let you do that,' she said. 'That was never part of the arrangement between us. Besides…' something elu-sive flickered in her expression, her voice '…there's the very generous settlement you offered for when… well, when our marriage ends.'

He watched her reach for her wine glass, noting the way her fingers—now with their beautifully mani-cured and painted nails—tightened around the stem.

'Well, there's a while till then,' he said evenly. 'But London would certainly be the best place when it comes to jobs. Are you still keen on finding something in publishing?'

'That would be lovely,' she said reflectively. 'But it's highly competitive, and I'm older than most new starters. And do I really want to be in London? It's fine occasionally—like now—but would I want to live here all the time?'

She gave a faint sigh, and Dante picked up on it.

'There's no rush to make your mind up. In fact,' he said slowly, 'what might be best for you right now is to take a complete break. Your time at the resort obviously did you good—so why not continue to broaden your horizons?'

He let his eyes rest on her. Deep inside, he could feel that low, dark purr start again. It was even lower now, and deeper. More disturbing to his peace of mind. He knew he should be helping Connie make her mind up about what to do next with her life, helping her move forward. Knew, too, that the makeover she'd indulged in was primarily for her own benefit.

Not mine.

And yet…

Instinctively his eyes went to her, rested on her. Taking in the extraordinary change in her appearance. He didn't want to be shallow…didn't want to be predictable. He knew perfectly well that there was a lot more to Connie than just the way she looked. He'd known it since he'd met her. He knew that he already liked her for who she was—not what she looked like.

And yet…

The pause came again—more potent this time. He'd been stunned by the difference her makeover had made, and had been open in his appreciation of the difference in her—not just physically, but emotionally—and totally honest in his compliments. He wanted her to bask in the moment after all she'd been through.

And yet…

There it was again. Pushing itself into his consciousness, despite his best endeavours not to give it house room. Not to claim it for himself, greedily and selfishly. But now, as he noticed how very lovely Connie looked sitting there, he knew with a certainty that was coming from deep inside him that the way he was responding to her was very, very personal.

And he knew the name of it. Knew the name of what had never been between them—what had nothing at all to do with their marriage or their relationship, their friendship, up to this point.

But it was there now. Rich and potent and growing more powerful with every moment that he let his gaze rest on the long-lashed cerulean depths of her eyes, on the delicate curve of her cheek softened by the wisping tendrils from her upswept hair, on the sweet contours of her mouth…

He felt it quicken within him and knew it for what it was, and what he could not deny. Could only acknowledge and accept.

Desire…

* * *

'That was a truly superb meal,' Connie was saying with a smiling sigh. 'Worth every last calorie!'

Dante turned from sliding his key card down the lock on the door to their suite. 'I'm glad you enjoyed it,' he said. 'But Connie, I don't want you worrying about calories. You look fantastic, and I'm so pleased for you, but don't for a moment stint yourself over food—promise me?'

He ushered her inside the suite. He was still in something of a daze, trying to process what he was feeling for Connie. It had happened so suddenly. In one sense Connie was still exactly the same person he'd come to know in the months since they'd married each other. In another...

She is completely new—a revelation to me!

He tamped it down—which was the only safe thing to do right now. For his own sake and, more importantly, for Connie's.

Is she reacting to me the way I am to her?

He didn't know—couldn't tell. Knew only that he must tread very carefully.

'Coffee,' he said cheerfully. 'I ordered it from the restaurant. It should be waiting for us.'

It was—sitting on a tray on the low table in front of the sofa in the reception area of the suite. Connie went and sat down, giving a sigh of relief. Making a face, she bent to take her high heels off as Dante took his place on the sofa, ensuring he was not sitting too close to her. That would be risky.

'Oh, gosh, that feels so much better!' Connie exclaimed with a groan, flexing her stockinged feet.

They were narrow and elegant, Dante noted absently. Something else he'd never noticed about her yet was now burningly conscious of.

Like the way she's relaxing back against the cushions, her beautiful dress moulding her figure, rounding her breasts...

He dragged his gaze to the coffee tray, pouring for them both. Behind his smile as he handed her a cup his thoughts were teeming. The low pulse in his body was tangible. He needed to get a grip on his libido—not indulge it.

This is happening too suddenly.

He told himself to speak, find an innocuous subject, avert his eyes from the way her curves were on display, the way she was lazily, almost sensuously, flexing her feet and rotating her ankles while taking sips of her own coffee.

Does she have any idea of the impact she's having on me?

She was unconscious of it, he was sure. And that only made it all the more potent.

'So, did you buy any other fabulous outfits this afternoon?' he asked conversationally, hoping it would divert him.

'No, just this one,' she answered.

'Well, why not buy some more?' he suggested. 'London may not be Milan, but it's got plenty to offer fashion-wise. Let's go shopping tomorrow.'

She stirred her coffee, dropping her eyes. 'I ought to go home tomorrow,' she said quietly.

'Why?' said Dante. It was a blunt question, but it was asked instinctively. He didn't want her leaving him. Not now.

Not now that my eyes are opened to her. Now that things are changing between us. Now that I've realised I want them to change—and want her to want it too...

She went on drinking her coffee. Dante got the impression she was doing it to avoid looking at him.

'Well, I've been away for a long time,' she said at last. 'I ought to check on the cottage.'

'It can wait another day, can't it?' he replied. 'How about if we go shopping tomorrow,' he went on, 'then I drive us down to the cottage the day after?'

Her glance went to him then. 'Oh, you don't have to do that, Dante. I can take the train, no problem.'

'I'd like to,' he insisted. 'And anyway—'

He broke off and she looked at him, a puzzled expression on her face.

He set down his coffee cup. 'Connie, I mentioned earlier about you broadening your horizons. I've had an idea. While you're thinking about what you might want to do next, how about having a break away completely?'

He took a breath, held her eyes. The sense that she was hiding something came to him again, though she was looking at him straight on.

'Why not come back to Italy with me?'

He made it sound like a casual suggestion, though

there was nothing casual at all in what he was asking her. He knew perfectly well what the reason was.

'You saw nothing of it when you came after our wedding, but now—well, I can show you Milan, and Lombardy—show you all of Italy, if you'd like that?'

He was conscious of a growing enthusiasm in himself. Taking her back to Italy with him was exactly what he wanted to do!

He pressed his argument. 'You've been largely confined to the West Country, but now you can spread your wings if you want to.'

'Do...do you mean it, Dante?' Connie's voice sounded hesitant.

He met her gaze—it was questioning and uncertain. Met it full-on.

'Yes,' he said. And then it was his turn to sound questioning. 'Doesn't the idea appeal?'

He wanted it to appeal to her—he wanted it very badly. All evening the feeling had been growing, becoming insistent, demanding he recognise what was happening between them. That what he had with Connie was changing, becoming something new. Something he could not resist. Did not want to resist.

Did not want her to resist either...

He was looking straight at her, into her eyes, her beautiful, deep-set blue eyes, with their delicately arched brows and their incredibly long, thick lashes. Almost he reached out his hand to stroke the silky peach of her cheek...

He felt his wishes coalesce into one. That she should want what he wanted...that they should share all that was changing between them—all that he had realised about her.

Desire me, Connie—desire me as much I now know I desire you.

He saw her eyes change, become less shadowed. And suddenly they blazed.

'Oh, yes…' she breathed. 'Oh, Dante, yes—*yes*!'

Her eyes were shining now, widening, pouring into his like sapphire jewels. His breath caught. She was so beautiful, so incredibly, stunningly beautiful. So perfectly irresistible…

With a strength of will he had not known he possessed, he got to his feet. With another surge of iron willpower he kept his voice light, his smile only warm and friendly.

'Good,' he announced. He drained the rest of his coffee, set down the cup. 'So that's settled. Tomorrow we'll extend your wardrobe, and then we can head for Italy. Does that sound good?'

She hadn't moved, was still staring at him with those beautiful widened cerulean eyes. He felt desire stir within him.

No! He had to shut it down. Now. Right now.

'OK, finish your coffee, then it's time for bed. We've a full day ahead of us tomorrow. All that shopping… And we'll need to get your passport couriered here as well.'

She gave a shake of her head, and instantly Dante saw how it feathered the fall of her hair, bringing tendrils around her face so attractively…

'I've got it with me,' she said. 'It's a useful form of ID.'

She was getting to her feet, scooping up her high heels as she did so, holding them loosely in her hand. Her eyes were wide and shimmering, lips slightly parted, and her beautiful shapely body, sheathed by the silk of her dress, was so close to his that he could catch the scent of her perfume.

Did she seem to sway for a moment, gazing up at him with what he thought was desire in her eyes? It was making every muscle in his body tighten in anticipation... But Dante kept himself rooted to the spot, as if he were mentally driving spikes through his feet to keep himself there.

Don't look at me like that, Connie. Just don't! Because if you do...if you do...then...

His self-control held—just.

'Buona notte,' he said, keeping his voice firm and keeping an even firmer hold on his self-control.

To his abject relief she turned away, eyes dropping suddenly, heading towards her bedroom.

'Buona notte, Dante,' she echoed, and he would have had to be deaf not to hear what was in her voice.

Exactly the same emotion as had been in her shimmering gaze.

He drove those spikes through his feet deeper yet. He had to—just *had* to—hold on.

I can't rush her—not like this—however much I long to do so.

He watched her gain entrance to her room, and only then did he dare breathe. His gaze rested on the bedroom door she'd closed behind her. Closed against him.

I should go to my own room. Take a cold shower—as cold as I can bear.

Yes, that was what he should do. And he would do it. He must. He'd lift one foot off the ground, and then the other, and head to his own bedroom.

He didn't know how he did it, but he started to walk—purposefully, determinedly—towards the one place he should go. Right now...

Connie sat at the vanity unit in her bedroom, gazing at her reflection in the soft light above the mirror—the only light she'd put on in the bedroom. She'd slipped out of her dress—that beautiful, extravagant dress that had made her into someone completely different, someone she'd never known she could be—and hung it on one of the padded hangers in the wardrobe, lovingly smoothing her hand down the lustrous material.

Now she sat in her new, luxuriously silky lingerie, knowing she should head for the bathroom, get into her pyjamas and go to bed. But not just yet...

She was still reliving, moment by moment, how she'd walked into the cocktail bar and seen Dante catching sight of her. He was the most gorgeous man in all the world. He had been for her from the very first time she'd seen him. And in his eyes...in his frozen stillness...she'd seen what she had so longed to see in her secret dreams and fantasies. What she had crushed down, never admitted to, but what was somehow now wonderfully real.

What it might portend for her and Dante she set aside. She would think about that later. For now, she would just give herself to the moment…to the wonder and delight swirling within her.

That sense of wonderful, bemused delight had gone on all evening. All through drinks at the swish, swanky bar, and all through dinner in the swish, swanky restaurant, with its celebrity chef and hushed exclusivity and its no-prices-on-the-menu expensiveness.

That look in his eyes…in those dark, drowning, long-lashed eyes that did such delicious things to her…that look had never left him.

And she knew it for what it was—knew how glorious it was to see it in his gaze.

To be desired by Dante.

Her secret, impossible dream.

Which was seemingly no longer impossible…

Yearning filled her, and longing, and a soft, seductive quickening in her blood.

She could see it in her own reflection.

And she could see one thing more in the vanity mirror.

She could see that her bedroom door was opening, and Dante was standing there, framed against the light.

He could hear his heart thudding in his chest, feel the tightness in his lungs, in his whole body. Could hear his own protests inside his head that this was not what he should be doing, not where he should be.

Yet he knew with an overriding certainty that it was the only place he wanted to be.

He felt his breath catch as his eyes went to her, sitting at the vanity unit, pooled in golden light. And then, with a surging in his blood, he saw that she had taken off that incredible dress which did such fabulous things to her body and was seated in nothing more than a silky camisole and lacy panties.

His blood surged again, coursing through him, rampant and arousing.

He stepped forward blindly, instinctively.

She did not move. But her reflected gaze in the mirror met his full-on, clashed and melded and fused with it. He walked towards her, saying not a word. No words were necessary. He stood behind her, looking down at her, and slowly…infinitely slowly…placed his hands on her almost bare shoulders.

Then, and only then, he said her name.

And she said his.

The touch of his hands on her shoulders, then grazing the delicate nape of her neck with his fingertips, sent sheets of exquisite sensation through her. She gave a shiver, a quiet moan emanating from deep in the throat his fingers were now brushing. He was standing so close behind her that she could catch his heat, his scent, his eyes holding hers in the reflection of the glass.

Faintness drummed through her. Melting her. Dissolving her.

He said her name again, his voice husky. She felt

herself rise to her feet, lift her face to him. Her breath caught. In his eyes was a blaze that set her aflame.

His mouth descended, caressing hers with the lightest, sweetest touch. Instinctively her arms wound around his neck, pulling him close against her. The hard wall of his chest pressed the cresting peaks of her breasts, engendering in her such an arousal of her senses that it was as if she'd been drinking strong, heady wine.

His kiss deepened, and he crushed her to him. With a little shiver of shock—of newly rising eagerness— she felt the evidence of his desire for her. A rush went through her…a sensual excitement that was like a forest fire within her.

His fingers were sliding down the narrow straps of her chemise and the bra beneath, sliding them from her body, freeing her swollen, sensitive breasts. Holding her shoulders, he dipped his head, and with a catch in her throat, her head tilting back, she felt his mouth close over their rounded orbs. Sensation after sensation speared her. Her own desire was quickening, answering his. She wanted more—oh, so much more.

As if answering her unspoken plea, he slipped the rest of her skimpy underwear from her body, discarding it on the floor. Then he started on his own unwanted clothes. She could hear his heavy breathing. His eyes never left her, the hunger in them blatant as she stood there in the low light.

Naked for him.

Waiting for him.

Waiting for him to make her his.

It was the most glorious feeling in the world…

Her eyes feasted on him—on the smooth, strong expanse of his muscular chest, on the narrowness of his lithe hips. On the proof of his desire for her.

He saw the direction of her gaze. Gave an amused chuckle, soft and sensual, that sent another dart of excitement through her.

Then he was taking her hand, leading her to the bed. And the sheet was cool on her back against her heated skin. Restlessly, filled with an urgency that was shooting through her veins, she reached for him as he slipped into bed beside her. She wanted him so much, so desperately…

She said his name, and in her voice was all her plea, all her desire. He gave another wicked little laugh, deep in his throat, his eyes pouring into hers.

'I wanted to give you time,' he said hoarsely. 'Time to realise what you were doing to me.'

She wound her arms around his neck, glorying in it. '*This* is the time,' she said. And drew his mouth down to hers.

He came over her, and the weight of his hard, naked body was all that she'd ever wanted to feel. She had longed for the strength of his arousal, his desire for her, for so long, and here it was now. *Now* was the time for his desire for her. *Now*, as his hands shaped her breasts, her waist, her flanks, slid down between her thighs, which parted with an instinct old as time to let him reach where she ached most for his touch.

She gave a helpless moan as he drew from her the

wonder of what her aching body was capable of feeling. It was exquisite, ecstatic, sensual, and it was giving her a hunger for him, a desperation, an urgency for more, and more, and more…

Restlessly, she widened her legs further, tightening her arms around him. She wanted…and craved…and longed for everything he could give her. She said his name again—a helpless plea, a yearning, an invitation—with desire in her voice…

She felt him lift his body away from hers and gave a cry of desolation. But then he was coming down on her again and now… Oh… Her neck arched back, her hips instinctively lifted, and she was receiving him, taking him into her, fusing her body with his, making them one, melding herself with him, and he with her.

She cried out as sensation exploded within her. Wave after wave after wave…convulsing her body around his. And in the tsunami of pleasure overwhelming her she heard him cry out too, hoarse and triumphant, and then the wave was possessing them both…endlessly, eternally.

Suddenly she knew that she was his, and he was hers, and that giving herself to him with all her being, all her heart, was everything she could ever want.

Dante.

Her Dante.

Hers…

Connie woke and curved her body into Dante's, revelling in the closeness of their embrace. His arm was still thrown over her, enfolding her, her back to his front, and her head was nestled against his strong chest. Their legs were tangled together, heavy and inert. The rest of the world did not exist. Only her and Dante. Dante and her…

She felt him stir slightly as she moved, then subside again, as she did, sleep calling to her once more, heavy and somnolent, warm and embracing. She gave a sigh of sweetest contentment and drifted off again… dreaming of Dante as she had dreamt so hopelessly for so long.

Now—magically, wondrously, ecstatically—it was a hopeless dream no longer.

But one filled instead with the sweetest bliss…

CHAPTER FIVE

DANTE STOOD THERE, looking down at the woman so peacefully asleep, her breathing quiet and even, her dusky eyelashes brushing her cheeks, one lock of hair curved around her shoulder.

For a while he just went on looking and wondering.

Had last night really happened? The most unexpected thing in all the world?

This time yesterday I had no idea—none!—that I'd be standing here this morning, gazing down at Connie like this.

For a moment—just a moment—doubt washed through him. Not doubt that last night really had happened, regardless of what he'd just thought—because it was impossible to doubt that with the evidence in front of his eyes—but doubt as to whether it should have happened at all.

I rushed it! I told myself I mustn't—but in the end I just could not resist her.

Compunction smote him—but only for a moment. Connie was stirring, as if aware of his gaze upon her, and she opened her eyes, blinking in the morning light, her gaze going straight to him.

Radiance suffused her face, telling him, with the blazing delight and wonder in her eyes, that what had happened last night had been as impossible for her to resist as for him. Gladness filled him, banishing all doubt, sweeping all feelings of compunction—so obviously and thankfully unnecessary—into oblivion.

He lowered himself to sit down on the bed, leaning forward to kiss Connie softly on her parted lips. 'Good morning,' he murmured, lifting his head away, and holding her gaze. 'Are you ready for breakfast?'

She didn't answer immediately, only went on gazing up at him—as though she doubted he were really there…as though he was all she ever wanted to look at. Her eyes glowed sapphire, luminous and revealing. Too revealing?

Dante got to his feet, tugging his dressing gown more tightly around him.

'Don't look at me like that,' he said, with wry humour in his voice, knowing she had no idea just how powerfully that candid gaze of hers worked on him. 'Or breakfast might have to wait a bit longer.'

He headed for the ensuite bathroom of her bedroom, knowing how close he'd come to showing her just why breakfast would have to wait. He lifted down the towelling bathrobe and brought it across to her.

'Your robe, milady,' he said lightly, and draped it on the bed. Then he crossed to the door. 'See you shortly—breakfast is on its way.'

He didn't want to see her put the towelling robe

on, covering all her beautiful silky skin—that, too, might delay breakfast for quite a while.

He made it out of the room, moving to the large window overlooking the rooftops of London. He was trying to understand what his feelings were, to make sense of all that was going through him, but all he knew was that taking Connie into his arms, into his intimate embrace, had been like nothing and no one he had ever known before. She was like no other woman in his life.

Because I know her. I have spent time with her, getting to know her, our lives are linked together. We already have something between us—warmth, familiarity, friendship, companionship—and that makes everything feel...

Different.

Just why or how exactly, he didn't know. It was new to him—quite new.

And special.

That was the word that came to him, even though he could not define it, or explain it, or understand it, as he turned at hearing her come into the room. His face broke into a smile, encompassing her totally, and the blazing radiance of her answering smile sent him reeling.

His gaze feasted on her. In the morning light she looked as lovely as she had last night, but in a totally different way. She was not the stunningly glamorous creature she had appeared to be last night, done up to the nines, but she had a kind of soft sensuality about her, with her tousled hair, her sleepy gaze, her

"One Minute" Survey

You get up to **FOUR** books
<u>and</u> a Mystery Gift...

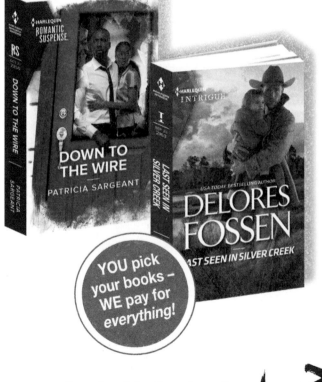
See inside for details.

Dear Reader,

Your opinions are important to us. So if you'll participate in our fast and free "One Minute" Survey, YOU can pick up to four wonderful books that WE pay for when you try the Harlequin Reader Service!

As a leading publisher of women's fiction, we'd love to hear from you. That's why we promise to reward you for completing our survey.

IMPORTANT: Please complete the survey and return it. We'll send your Free Books and a Free Mystery Gift right away. And we pay for shipping and handling too! ← *We pay for EVERYTHING!*

Try **Harlequin® Romantic Suspense** and get 2 books featuring heart-racing page-turners with unexpected plot twists and irresistible chemistry that will keep you guessing to the very end.

Try **Harlequin Intrigue® Larger-Print** and get 2 books featuring action-packed stories that will keep you on the edge of your seat. Solve the crime and deliver justice at all costs.

Or TRY BOTH!

Thank you again for participating in our "One Minute" Survey. It really takes just a minute (or less) to complete the survey… and your free books and gift will be well worth it!

If you continue with your subscription, you can look forward to curated monthly shipments of brand-new books from your selected series, always at a discount off the cover price! Plus you can cancel any time. So don't miss out, return your One Minute Survey today to get your Free books.

Pam Powers

"One Minute" Survey

GET YOUR FREE BOOKS AND A FREE GIFT!
✓ Complete this Survey ✓ Return this survey

◀ **DETACH AND MAIL CARD TODAY!** ▶

1 Do you try to find time to read every day?
☐ YES ☐ NO

2 Do you prefer stories with suspensful storylines?
☐ YES ☐ NO

3 Do you enjoy having books delivered to your home?
☐ YES ☐ NO

4 Do you share your favorite books with friends?
☐ YES ☐ NO

YES! I have completed the above "One Minute" Survey. Please send me my Free Books and a Free Mystery Gift (worth over \$20 retail). I understand that I am under no obligation to buy anything, as explained on the back of this card.

☐ **Harlequin® Romantic Suspense**
240/340 CTI G2AD

☐ **Harlequin Intrigue® Larger-Print**
199/399 CTI G2AD

☐ **BOTH**
240/340 & 199/399 CTI G2AE

FIRST NAME | LAST NAME

ADDRESS

APT.# | CITY

STATE/PROV. | ZIP/POSTAL CODE

EMAIL ☐ Please check this box if you would like to receive newsletters and promotional emails from Harlequin Enterprises ULC and its affiliates. You can unsubscribe anytime.

HI/HRS-1123-OM

▲ If offer card is missing write to: Harlequin Reader Service, P.O. Box 1341, Buffalo, NY 14240-8531 or visit www.ReaderService.com ▲

BUSINESS REPLY MAIL
FIRST-CLASS MAIL PERMIT NO. 717 BUFFALO, NY

POSTAGE WILL BE PAID BY ADDRESSEE

HARLEQUIN READER SERVICE
PO BOX 1341
BUFFALO NY 14240-8571

NO POSTAGE
NECESSARY
IF MAILED
IN THE
UNITED STATES

bee-stung mouth and the way the lapels of her tow-elling robe were quite insufficient in concealing the generosity of her cleavage...

The doorbell pinged and he was relieved: break-fast was arriving. The business of the suite's butler, the laden trolley, getting themselves seated and all the dishes set out or set to keep warm on chafing trays, seemed to take for ever, but at last they were on their own again. His eyes were on her the whole time as they got stuck in to the lavish breakfast in front of them. And her gaze on him was constant, glowing, filling him with warmth.

A warmth which, when they were finally replete, Dante took ruthless advantage of.

'There's no rush to hit the shops,' he told her, tak-ing her hand, knowing his voice was huskily sugges-tive and his eyelids were drooping with quickening desire.

She meshed her fingers with his, saying nothing, letting him lead her to where he wanted her to be.

Her bed. With him. Making love to her again. And then again...

In Italy, they didn't intend to spend very much time in Milan. Just long enough for Dante to touch base with his office, clear his diary—to the obvious sur-prise of his staff—and whisk Connie off to the fabled Quadrilatero area of the city, where the most famous fashion houses were based.

Though it was with wide-eyed wonder that she tried on the gorgeous creations, Connie was resistant to allowing Dante to buy too much for her, on top of what he'd bought her in London.

'I feel bad accepting what you've already bought for me,' she told him ruefully.

He looked taken aback. Then kissed her forehead indulgently. 'It is my pleasure,' he said.

But she still shook her head. Of course she wanted to look as stunning as possible for Dante, now that she finally felt so good about her body—but not at his expense. They bickered about it good-naturedly, and Connie compromised by agreeing that when they returned to Milan she might go shopping again.

But first they were going on holiday.

Again, Connie had initially demurred. 'Dante, I don't want to drag you away from your work. I know how important it is to you,' she'd said anxiously.

Again, he'd dropped an indulgent kiss on her forehead.

'It is my pleasure,' he had said to this objection too.

Now he drew her closer to him on the massive sofa that was the centrepiece of the living area of his apartment in Milan. It was a ferociously modern apartment, and it was so very strange to Connie for her to be here again.

The only time she'd been there before had been immediately after their wedding, and they'd spent only two nights there. She'd been anxious about leaving her grandmother for too long, and Dante had been anxious about his grandfather's lawyers, whom they'd had to call upon, vital marriage certificate in hand, to demonstrate his new eligibility for his inheritance.

Dante had been tense and preoccupied, and Connie had kept as quiet as possible, stayed as unobtrusive as she could. It had been an awkward visit, ramming home to her the sheer weirdness of what she had done—marrying a complete stranger for the reasons she had.

'To getting what we want...'

That toast Dante had given on the private jet was in her head again. And, oh, how different it was to hear it now!

She snuggled into him, feeling his strong shoulder under her head, and gave a happy sigh. On that brief, awkward former visit she had, of course, slept in the guest bedroom. Now, as she lifted her face to Dante, who met her ardent gaze with one of his own, it was entirely, utterly different.

Happiness surged through her. Back then, Dante had been as far beyond her as if he were on the moon. She might have looked, and gazed, and yearned... but that was all.

But now she was here with him because he wanted her to be here, and no longer as the stranger he'd had to marry and wished he hadn't.

Now he desires me passionately...irresistibly... He wants me in his life. Wants to be with me and wants me to be with him.

She saw his expression change as she gazed up at him, her body moulded against his. She felt his arm around her shoulder tighten, his eyelids start to droop. Saw his mouth start to lower to hers...felt the first feathering velvet touch of his lips. She answered it with hers, her fingers splayed deliciously against the hard, muscled wall of his chest.

In moments the rest of the world had faded away and there was only her and Dante, Dante and her, and their bodies craving each other, their desire like a flame. Then he was scooping her up, carrying her to his bedroom—*their* bedroom—to his bed—*their* bed.

And time, as well as the world, vanished.

Dante parked the car at the ferry dock and glanced across at Connie. 'Nearly there now,' he said.

'Nearly *where*?' Connie asked with humorous demand.

'You'll see.'

That was all Dante would offer her. It was only once they were aboard the waiting ferry that he relented.

'We're heading for one of the islands that make-up the Tuscan Archipelago.'

Connie's eyebrows rose. 'I've never heard of the Tuscan Archipelago,' she exclaimed.

'The most famous island is Elba,' Dante elucidated. 'We can visit while we're on holiday if you're interested. It was where Napoleon was first exiled. But the island we're going to is much smaller. Cars are very restricted—only allowed for deliveries and local essentials, not for tourists.' He paused. 'I hope you'll like it. It's very quiet and sleepy and old-fashioned, but that, I think, is its appeal.'

'It sounds idyllic. I'm sure I'll love it,' Connie assured him.

* * *

It was the answer Dante wanted. He'd chosen their destination specifically because he'd thought it might best suit Connie's obvious love of 'old' in general. She was polite about his apartment in Milan, but it was clear that her tastes had been moulded by her grandmother's little Victorian cottage, and he was happy to indulge her when on holiday.

Besides, the island had one other salient virtue. It wasn't fashionable in the least—which meant he was highly unlikely to run into anyone he knew. And that meant he could have Connie entirely to himself.

Just the way he wanted her.

Thoughts flickered in his head, trying to be heard, but he dismissed them. He didn't want them there, disturbing what he had with Connie.

What I never in a million years thought I would ever have!

In the middle of the night he would still wake sometimes, with Connie naked in his arms, embracing her lovely body—trimmer now, and more toned because of her healthier diet and her exertions in the gym, but still soft and rounded and deliciously curvy—and find himself stunned at what had happened.

But it had happened, and he was simply going with it. It wasn't in the least what he'd imagined was even a possibility, but here it was—and he was giving himself to it completely. Right now, it was all he wanted.

His gaze went to her now, drawing away from the azure sea. Watching the little island get closer, Connie leant on the ferry's railings, the breeze winnowing her hair. She was a knockout, as ever, in stylish navy blue trousers and a loose-knit jersey top, looking relaxed and happy.

He draped an arm around her back and she turned her face to his, smiling at his touch.

'Do you know the island we're going to?' she asked. 'Have you been before?'

He shook his head. 'No, it's not somewhere I'd think of doing business.' His expression changed. 'Most of what I've seen of my own country—let alone any others—has generally been for business reasons.'

It sounded rather depressing, said out loud like that, and he gave a shrug to dispel the feeling. 'So this will be a real change for me,' he added, his voice lightening.

Connie smiled up at him again, then went back to gazing at the horizon. 'It's so gorgeous being out at sea like this,' she said. 'The sun on the water...the breeze in my hair.'

'If you like,' he said, 'we can hire a motorboat and take off around the island. There are little bays and remote rocky coves...we can go snorkelling.' His eyes glinted. 'Even skinny dipping, perhaps?'

She gave a laugh. 'They'd have to be *very* remote coves for that!' she warned. She looked at him again. 'Where are we going to be staying, by the way? Or is that a secret too?'

Dante shook his head. 'No, not at all. I've rented a beach villa a little way out of the main town—the only town. It's not luxurious, but it looked good online, so I hope it won't disappoint. There's a decent hotel in town, if you'd prefer.'

'A beach villa sounds perfect,' Connie said enthusiastically. 'Can we do barbies on the beach?'

'I'm sure we can. And if we get bored we'll stroll into town and eat at some of the restaurants—there are a good few. Many of the people who come to the island do so on day trips, either from the larger islands or from the mainland, so the place caters for visitors.'

'It all sounds absolutely lovely!' Connie exclaimed.

Dante's arm tightened around her and he went back to gazing out over the water at the approaching island, pointing out the harbour they could already see at the far end of the little town that curved around the sweep of the bay.

It was not long before the ferry docked and they were disembarking. A few taxis waited, but Dante had a different means of transport in mind, as he told Connie.

'Bicycles?' she guessed.

He gave a laugh. 'Not right now—but we can hire them if you like, to explore the island. No, our transport is just there.'

He pointed to the edge of the quay and Connie gave a squeal of delight. 'A pony and trap!'

'Trap?' echoed Dante, nonplussed.

'A small horse-drawn carriage,' Connie explained. 'I've no idea why it's called a trap.'

They walked across to it. Dante pulled their suitcases, which he hefted up into the trap. The driver—an ancient individual with an even more ancient straw hat—said something to him in a strong dialect, raising his whip in greeting.

Meanwhile Connie had gone to meet and greet the steed who would be doing all the work. Not a pony, but a placid-looking working horse, also wearing a straw hat to protect him against the sun, his long ears poking through. Dante saw her speak affectionately to him and stroke his velvet nose, at which he whickered softly.

'All aboard,' said Dante cheerfully.

His mood was excellent. Connie was on board with his choice for their holiday, the sun was shining but a sea breeze freshened the heat, and now they were about to head for their private beach villa—very private!

He helped Connie up and they moved off at a sedate walking pace. Dante didn't mind the slowness. It gave him time to look about with Connie as they made their way along what was, effectively, the main road of the little town, along the seafront.

The houses and restaurants and café-bars along the way were old-fashioned-looking, with wooden shutters and faded pastel-painted fronts and walls. The whole place had an unhurried, sleepy feel to it. The ancient driver greeted various acquaintances in almost unintelligible tones as they progressed, and Connie gave a laugh.

'I feel I ought to wave at them. You know—like the Queen? All very gracious. And maybe nod my head as well!'

'Go ahead.' Dante gave an answering laugh. 'Who knows? They may take us for royalty.'

He stretched out his legs, relaxing completely, feeling his good mood increasing. This was going to be an excellent holiday...

And so it proved. The beach villa was simple, yes, but with all that was needed—including a brick-built barbecue, just as Connie had wished for. It was ideal, and only a few steps from a small and secluded beach. There was no pool—but who needed a pool when the clear, calm azure waters awaited them?

Dante found himself wondering whether any female he'd ever run around with before would have condescended to stay in so quiet and rustic a destination. But Connie was like no other woman he knew— and she clearly loved it here.

So did he.

The days passed in easy succession—undemanding, totally relaxing—and Dante gave himself over to them. Work seemed a million miles away, and he was glad of it. Internet connection was not great, and he was glad of that too. It gave him a good reason not to let himself be plagued by his office.

And why should he be? He had competent staff, and in the time since his grandfather had died he'd overseen the smooth transfer to his own executive control, adding in some of his key people, letting some of his grandfather's retire, but without any acrimony. The company was making even more money than when his grandfather had been in charge, and all the years of dogged apprenticeship he'd put in as his grandfather's heir had trained him completely to do what was necessary.

His thoughts sheared away. He wasn't here to think about work. He was here to have what he had very seldom had before—a holiday. A solid two weeks—not just a few days snatched out of a hectic work schedule and invariably including some business meetings, even if he had managed to bring one of his fleeting *inamoratas* with him for the duration.

Both holidays and *inamoratas* were not something his grandfather had approved of.

Well, he thought defiantly, he was enjoying both right now.

Then a frown creased his brow, his eyes shifting to Connie, lying basking in the heat on her sun lounger beside him, face-down, the sculpted line of her back bared courtesy of her undone bikini top. How very lovely she looked…

And she was no *inamorata*, was she?

His gaze flickered. Connie was the woman he'd undergone a brief, hurried wedding ceremony with—the woman who had made it possible for him to claim his inheritance.

'*Inamorata*' was not the correct term to apply to her. She was far more than that.

His former flings had never lasted long. But why? He remembered telling Raf that because his grandfather had worked him so hard he'd never damn well had time to build a relationship with anyone. Was that why any affair he'd started had never lasted?

Or was it because I never wanted them to last?

And if that was so, then why?

His expression tightened. A shrink might say it was because of his parents...the fact that they'd been killed when he was only a boy. But how did that tie in—if it even did? Or was it because he had bought into his grandfather's obsession with work? Leaving no time for anything else? Or was it because it had been bad enough that his grandfather had controlled his life, and letting a woman do that too would have been intolerable?

There was a shadow in his eyes now, and a memory plucked at him of how fiercely he'd rejected the idea of picking one of his exes to marry to meet the terms of the will, on the grounds that no female he knew would be prepared to make so temporary a marriage. They'd have wanted to tie him down...curb the freedom he'd never even had the chance to enjoy...

That, after all, was what had made Connie so ideal as his wife. She had no interest in a permanent marriage. Not then, when he'd married her, and not now either.

He felt a sense of relief go through him. This was exactly why he and Connie got on so well. And what was happening between them now—amazing as it was—didn't change any of that.

We're just enjoying ourselves...having a wonderful time. Friends who have quite unexpectedly become lovers—for now.

Yes, that was the way to look at it—that made sense. And now that it did his expression changed, became lighter. He could put his concerns aside and just get on with enjoying this time with Connie while it lasted. There were several months ahead still to enjoy. That was good—very good.

A feeling of intense satisfaction filled him. He reached his hand across to her as he put all complicated thoughts out of his head. He didn't want complications. He wanted what he was having now.

A holiday. Relaxation. An easy time.

And Connie.

Oh, he most definitely wanted Connie...

In bed and out. By day and by night.

And right now, too.

He gave a wry smile. Though they wouldn't be up for anything too passionate in this heat...

He let his fingers run lazily down the length of her spine. She stirred at his touch, stretching languorously.

'Time for a cool-down swim,' Dante said. 'Then lunch.'

'Sounds good,' she said, retying her bikini top.

'You could always try going topless,' Dante remarked. His eyes glinted hopefully.

He got an old-fashioned look as his reward, and laughed, contenting himself with helping her lever herself up from the lounger and head down to the water's edge.

The swim have them an appetite, and they ate *al fresco* on the villa's shady terrace, tucking into fresh bread, ham, cheese, tomatoes and peaches. Simple, but delicious. Tonight they were going to stroll into town and try out another of the restaurants along the seafront…

Over dinner, washed down with a local wine, tasty and robust, listening to the lapping of the sea against the harbour wall, they discussed the next day's delights.

'How about crossing over to Elba tomorrow?' Dante ventured, glancing at Connie. 'Giving ourselves a dose of Napoleonic history?'

Connie's face lit up. 'Oh, yes, let's! Is there a ferry, or shall we take the motorboat across? Can you manage that distance?'

'Let's get ourselves taken over, shall we? I'm sure we can find a pilot. That way we can make a day of it.'

'Sounds good,' Connie said. 'So, tell me about Elba? I know Napoleon was first exiled there, and then managed to escape and get back to France in time for Waterloo, but that's about all…'

Dante had sounded forth with what he himself knew, but it was all amplified hugely by their visit.

'It's really too much to absorb in only one day's visit,' Connie said sadly. 'I hadn't realised Boney had *two* residences here—and we haven't time to see both.'

'Well, we'll just have to come back another time— have a holiday here, on Elba, and do it at our leisure,' Dante said easily, and the notion sounded attractive.

'That would be lovely,' Connie said.

But there was a quality to her voice that Dante

could not interpret. He wondered at it for a moment, then dismissed it.

'Let's get a coffee,' he said. 'History always makes me thirsty.'

She laughed. 'Considering that Italy is absolutely *full* of history—from the Etruscans onwards—you must be perpetually thirsty!'

He gave an answering laugh, putting his arm around her waist as they strolled towards a likely-looking café not far from Napoleon's town villa—now a museum, which they'd just visited.

It was good to put his arm around Connie, to have her close to him, to stroll along with her, amiably and leisurely, in an easy-going way. It was very relaxing to be with her, he mused. Probably because she lived life at a slower pace than he customarily did in his work-focused existence.

She gives me more time to appreciate things.

And he appreciated the present—this relaxing, getting-away-from-it-all holiday, this time with Connie, who had become what he had never before envisaged having at his side or in his life. Yes, it was good—definitely, unquestionably good.

They settled themselves down at a pavement table, under the café's striped awning, and ordered coffee. Dante, feeling peckish as well as in need of a caffeine shot after so much Napoleonic history, ordered a pastry as well.

Connie looked at it enviously.

Dante lazily pushed the plate towards her. 'Indulge,' he said genially.

She shook her head, reluctantly. 'Tempting—but not as tempting as you, Dante,' she said. 'I don't want to put all that weight I shifted straight back on and find you don't fancy me any longer!'

She spoke lightly—humorously, even—but Dante didn't want her thinking such thoughts even for a moment. They were totally unnecessary.

He retrieved the pastry, deliberately cut off the end and, forking it up, presented it to Connie.

'Let's test that theory out, shall we? You eat this, and I'll tell you if I still want to take you to bed. Then I'll eat the rest, and you can tell me if *you* still want to take *me* to bed. Fair enough?'

She gave a laugh. 'OK, you win,' she said, and helped herself to the cream-filled sliver of flaky pastry. 'Mmm… Oh, yes, that is good.' She sighed happily.

Dante's eyes rested on her. 'I can confirm,' he said with mock solemnity, 'that, yes, I definitely, definitely still want to take you to bed. In fact…' a husky note entered his voice '…if you like, we could spend the night here on Elba. Book into a hotel right away…'

She threw him a wicked glance. 'But my toothbrush is at the beach villa,' she teased.

'Another can be purchased in this very town, I believe,' he riposted dryly. 'Together with toothpaste, so I am told.'

In the end they didn't spend the night on Elba, but took the motorboat back to their own island, piloted by an individual as ancient as the driver of the pony and trap, who knew the currents and the sea lanes expertly.

The sun was setting, bathing the sea with gold and fiery red, as Dante relaxed back with Connie, his arm around her shoulder, her head resting on his, the breeze tossing their hair and cooling their faces as they cruised over the darkening waters of the Tyrrhenian Sea.

'Can anything be more perfect than this?' Connie murmured.

Dante could hear the happiness in her voice. Feel it echoing inside him.

His arm around her shoulder tightened, holding her even closer to him.

It felt amazing…

CHAPTER SIX

CONNIE WAS CHOPPING vegetables for dinner, carefully following the Italian recipe displayed on the laptop propped up on the gleaming work surface of the kitchen in Dante's high-tech kitchen in Milan. She'd bought the ingredients that afternoon, and wanted to surprise Dante. It would be the first time she'd cooked for him.

They'd come back from their island idyll a few days ago. Dante had headed back into the office, and she was spending her days happily exploring Milan. So far Dante had always ordered food in for the evening meal. Not pizza or curry—something far more gourmet than that! But now she wanted to prove that she could produce an edible meal for him by herself. It seemed a wifely thing to do.

A memory drifted through her head from long ago. Watching, as a little girl, while her mother chopped vegetables for dinner. Her father would come in from work, kissing her mother affectionately, saying how hungry he was, how good a cook she was, and her mother would beam with pleasure, telling him about the recipe she was preparing.

Connie had watched them, feeling safe, secure, and her father had come across to her, scooping her up into a protective hug, telling her with a grin that he hoped she'd grow up to become as good a cook as her mum and then her husband would always love her, like he loved her mother...

She felt her mind flicker between the long-ago past and the vivid present.

As if on cue, she heard Dante letting himself into his apartment and she called out. 'I'm in the kitchen!'

He strolled in, looking gorgeous as he always did, whether he was wearing casual holiday clothing or, like now, a business suit. He came over and kissed her lightly on the cheek, then surveyed her culinary preparations ruefully.

'I hate to say this, but would this keep till tomorrow? We've been invited out to dinner,' he announced.

Had he looked somewhat taken aback to see her so domestically employed? she wondered. But she was happy to cook for him—more than happy.

The echo of her father's words so long ago sounded again...

'It's Raf,' Dante went on. 'He's in Milan tonight. Flown up from Rome on business. Says he's looking forward to seeing you again.'

'Oh,' said Connie.

She had wondered if she was going to be introduced to some of Dante's friends here in Milan. And she had no objection to seeing Rafaello. He was a close friend of Dante's, even if he did live in Rome.

When they arrived at the restaurant where they were meeting him, Connie was aware that she felt self-conscious. Though Dante often mentioned him, she hadn't seen Rafaello since being in Milan after the wedding. It hadn't been hard to pick up the fact that he'd thought Dante mad to marry her, though he'd been nothing but polite. Would he think differently now?

She gave a mental shrug. Even though he was Dante's friend, Rafaello's opinion was immaterial. Even so, it would be nice, for Dante's sake, to see appreciation in his friend's eyes at her new appearance—so very different from when they'd first met. Maybe he might finally consider her worthy of his friend, she thought a touch tartly.

Rafaello greeted her courteously—smoothly, even—but made no comment about her changed appearance.

The outfit she was wearing now could not have been more different from the tent-like blue dress she'd worn for her wedding. It was a cream two-piece, with a narrow skirt and a bolero-style bodice with delicate, self-coloured embroidery around the neckline and cuffs. Her hair was in a low chignon, with ornamental combs, and she'd applied her make-up with care.

Glancing around the upmarket restaurant at the other fashionable Milanese gathered there, she knew she passed muster and was glad of it.

They went straight to their table, Dante's arm coming protectively around her back. He was being very attentive, but there was an air of slight tension about him all the same. Maybe he, too, was conscious of the vast gulf in appearance between old Connie and new Connie…

Well, she was new Connie now, and she had no reason to feel anything but confidently assured in a place like this, knowing she looked like every other designer-clad female here.

Her expression softened. But she was infinitely more privileged than they were.

Because I have Dante.

'A little different from the trattorias we've been used to on holiday,' Dante remarked dryly, as they took their places at the table. 'Raf likes to dine in style,' he added with a wink.

'Trattorias aren't exactly your usual style either, my friend,' was Rafaello's cool reply. 'But perhaps things have changed since we last met…' His glance went between them. Veiled. Assessing. 'So where did you go on holiday?' he went on, his voice less cool, more simply enquiring.

Dante named the island in the Tuscan Archipelago and Rafaello raised his arched eyebrows. 'Definitely off the beaten track,' he murmured. 'But it's done you good—you're looking very relaxed, old friend.' His tone was warmer now as he continued, 'And that's good to see.'

He turned his attention to Connie, and when he spoke again his voice was sympathetic.

'I was sorry to hear about the death of your grandmother—please accept my condolences.'

It was sincerely said, and Connie felt her throat tighten, tears threaten. Immediately Dante took her hand, squeezing it comfortingly.

'Thank you,' she managed to say to Rafaello. His unreadable gaze had taken in Dante's protective gesture, she could see.

'I hope this move to Italy will help you adjust,' Rafaello went on. 'Tell me…have you seen much of Milan yet?'

'I've been exploring,' she said, her voice firmer now, 'while Dante's busy at the office. I've found the nearest food market, for a start. And I'm going to try out some recipes on Dante,' she added lightly.

'Very domestic,' Rafaello remarked, as if amused.

His glance went to his friend. He murmured something in Italian to him that Connie did not catch— only two words 'treasure' and 'wife'.

Dante did not answer, but Connie had the impression that he resented what Rafaello had said.

Rafaello seemed unperturbed, though, and simply went on smoothly, 'Once Connie has settled in you should do some entertaining,' he said. 'Your friends will want to meet her. They'll be glad to see something of you, too.' He turned to Connie. 'Dante has become a complete workaholic since he took over the reins from his late grandfather.' He nodded. 'That's why I was glad to hear he'd taken off with you on holiday. It's definitely done him good.'

The warmth was back in his voice, and Connie liked him for it.

'And it's good that you can now be here with him,' he added.

He sounded approving, and Connie liked him for that too.

She smiled widely. 'It's wonderful to be here,' she said, casting an affectionate glance at Dante. He seemed to be tense, though, and she wondered why.

But the waiter was approaching, and the sommelier, and they all paid attention to their menus for a while, making their choices.

Rafaello shut his with a decisive click. 'Champagne,' he announced, 'is definitely in order!'

When a bottle was promptly presented, and flutes filled, he raised his foaming glass to his dinner guests.

'To Signor and Signora Cavelli, so very full of surprises.' That sardonic light was in his dark eyes again. 'Welcome ones, of course,' he added. 'In fact...' Connie saw his glance go between them '...very welcome...'

Connie smiled a little uncertainly and took a sip of the beading liquid. At her side Dante also took a mouthful, but said nothing. There was a tightness around his mouth, and again she wondered why.

Then Rafaello was setting down his glass, addressing Dante directly. 'I mean it, my friend—I am glad to see what I am seeing.'

Abruptly Connie felt Dante relax. Relieved, she felt herself relax as well. Their first courses soon arrived, and as they all got stuck in Rafaello asked some questions about their holiday. She and Dante answered readily, enthusiastically reminiscing, capping each other's recollections.

She was aware of Rafaello's shrewd gaze, but it no longer seemed to be assessing. If anything, it was amusedly approving. Presumably, she thought absently, because he'd originally been wary of Dante's choice of wife and now he could see just how happy they were.

Because Dante *was* happy. She knew it with absolute certainty. And she was so glad of it. A wash of that very same emotion went through her, and her eyes grew misty. Did she feel Rafaello looking at her? Well, he was welcome—more than welcome—to see how happy she was…how happy Dante was.

How happy we both are together.

The evening wore on and became increasingly convivial. Connie relaxed, enjoying the occasion. The gourmet food was beyond superb, and even if she could not appreciate the vintage wines as they should be appreciated, she certainly enjoyed them. Conversation was easy. Rafaello regaled her with tales of Rome, and she and Dante told him of their plans to tour the north of Italy, taking in new places every weekend.

'Well, don't wear Connie out,' Rafaello said, and smiled at Dante. 'And make some time for socialising in Milan too. Like I said, your friends haven't seen you out and about for a long time.'

'Connie prefers sightseeing,' Dante replied.

Was his voice tighter? Connie wondered. Perhaps he didn't like the suggestion that he was forcing her to go jaunting about, when the very opposite was true.

It was she who didn't want Dante feeling he had to show her the sights. But he seemed as keen on it as she was, and that was both reassuring and delightful. Just being with Dante was all she wanted. Her dream come true...

Her eyes went to Dante and softened as they always did. She felt her heart rate quicken. Emotion filled her with a rich, sweet warmth, setting her aglow.

A burst of Italian sounded behind her. Excited and voluble. She didn't understand a word of it.

Except one.

'Dante!'

She saw Rafaello look up sharply, and felt Dante stiffen beside her. She turned her head, as more Italian sounded.

'Dante! Mi caro! Che bello verderti! E passato cosi tanto!'

The speaker was gushing—there was no other word for it. And she looked exactly the kind of woman to gush.

Connie stared. Blonde, incredibly slender, tall like a model, she was wearing, Connie could instantly see, an outfit that had come from a top Milan fashion house. The woman stooped on her six-inch heels and swooped an air kiss down on Dante's cheek. Rafaello and Connie she completely ignored.

Connie's eyes went to Dante. His face had become expressionless, although he'd got to his feet politely.

'Bianca,' he greeted her, and took his seat again.

In front of Connie's eyes, the woman—Bianca—

helped herself to the fourth chair at their table, and gushed again, targeting Dante with more Italian that Connie did not understand.

Then, as if belatedly aware of her and Rafaello's presence, she turned towards them, bestowing a dazzling smile upon them.

'E Rafaello Ranieri, vero? Ci siamo conosciuti, ma credo in Roma—'

The smile widened to encompass Connie now.

'E tu sei l'ultima fidanzata di Rafaello? Che bello!'

Then, dismissing them again, she returned her lavish attentions to Dante, blatantly touching his cheek as if in reproach, her voice becoming sorrowful. Connie guessed that Bianca was lamenting the fact that Dante had been depriving himself of her affection. She could see Dante's expression freezing, his eyes darkening, but it was Rafaello who interjected.

He spoke in English. 'There's a slight misunderstanding here, I'm afraid. Connie is not with me—she is with Dante.' His voice was cool.

Immediately the blonde's expression changed. An openly hostile look was flashed towards Connie.

'Since when?' she demanded bluntly, eyes narrowing. She too, spoke in English now.

'Since they were married,' Rafaello answered, his voice icy now.

'Sposato?'

Another volley of Italian broke from the blonde, and then she pushed back the chair she'd commandeered and bolted to her feet. The look she threw at Connie was pure poison.

As for Dante, he'd gone completely rigid, his expression steeled. But not because of Bianca, Connie realised with an awareness that came to her at a level she could not explain.

Because of Rafaello.

The blonde threw one last angry word at Dante, then stalked off. Connie stared at Dante—then at Rafaello. Not understanding. Not wanting to understand. Something was passing between the two men—something that was registering in Dante as a rigid tension and in Rafaello as a studied coolness.

Dimly, something occurred to her.

He said that deliberately—about Dante being married to me.

But why was Dante reacting like this? They *were* married. So why—?

'Thanks, Raf,' Dante said bitingly, casting daggers at his friend. 'Bianca Delamondi is the very last damn person I would have wanted to know that!'

He glared furiously at Rafaello, but his friend, Connie could see, was sublimely unconcerned.

'It seemed the quickest way of getting rid of her,' he said, calmly reaching for his coffee cup and draining it. Then he glanced at his watch. 'I'd better call it a night,' he said, in the same unruffled manner. 'I'm on a morning flight to Palermo. An elderly client is being sued for divorce by his much younger second wife, and is objecting to her financial claims,' he said lightly, but with a discernible touch of cynicism. 'I must see what I can do to protect his money from her.'

'You do that,' Dante said shortly. 'It's what you're

best at.' His voice was tight. 'That and shooting your mouth off!'

The only response he got was a laugh from Rafaello as he summoned the bill for their dinner.

Connie felt awkward. Currents were running, and she did not fully understand them.

As if conscious of her disquiet, Rafaello threw her a half-amused look. 'Do not be alarmed—Dante and I have been sparring with each other since we were teenagers. He runs hot and I run cold—it's why we're such good friends.'

Connie eyed him doubtfully. Dante still had that tense, closed-off look on his face.

The waiter approached, proffering *l'addizione* discreetly in a leather folder. Rafaello signed it off with a careless hand. Then he turned to smile at his guests, encompassing them both.

'I'm so glad to have met you again, Connie—it has been such a delight.'

He helped himself to Connie's hand, and before she'd quite realised what he was intending he lifted it to his lips, kissing it with a Latin flourish before releasing it.

'And I very much hope that my old friend appreciates just what a gem he has in you.' His voice was drier now, and she saw him throw a challenging glance at Dante. 'I own I was concerned for him at first, having to make such a marriage, but no longer. You are doing him a great deal of good—more than he realises, I suspect.'

She could see Dante was glowering, but whether it

was because of the hand-kiss or what his friend had just said, she didn't know. In either case there was no need for him to look so dark, surely?

Then Rafaello was getting to his feet, taking his leave of them with a graceful *buono notte*.

When he had gone, Dante turned to Connie, taking her hand. His grip was enfolding.

'Raf can push my buttons sometimes,' he said tightly. 'He likes to think he knows me better than I know myself. As if!' His voice changed, and there was an apology in his eyes now. 'I'm sorry about Bianca,' he said frankly, with a rueful twist to his mouth.

Immediately Connie softened, felt the unease that Dante's tension had engendered in her dissipating. 'No need,' she assured him. 'I didn't understand what she was saying anyway.'

Dante gave a wry laugh. 'Just as well—she was referring to times past.'

Connie made herself give him an understanding look, to show she was not in the least embarrassed by this collision of Dante's past and his present. The blonde, ballistic Bianca would not be his only ex in Milan…

'But I could have done without Raf damn well shooting his mouth off.' Dante's voice had formed an edge again.

'Does…does it matter? Him saying that you're married to me?' Connie asked.

Uncertainty was filling her. Confusion. She wanted

him to say something reassuring, but his expression flickered, then became veiled.

'It's no one's business,' he said shortly. 'I've never worn a wedding band and nor have you. Our marriage and our reasons for marrying are private—our concern only, not anyone else's.'

Questions stabbed in Connie's head. Questions that were hardly formed, barely shaped, that could only articulate themselves into one single thought.

But everything's changed now—hasn't it?

Dante was getting to his feet and she did likewise, a sense of unease still plucking at her though she couldn't really say why. Surely there was no need for it?

He guided her out on to the pavement, where the restaurant's doorman was pulling a taxi over for them. As they got in, Dante took Connie's hand again, pressing it warmly, his thumb smoothing across her palm in a seductive manner.

His mood was clearly lifting, so Connie's did too.

'I can't wait to get home,' he said, turning to her, his voice low, with a rasp to it that Connie had learnt to recognise.

She gave a delicious shiver of anticipation and her sense of disquiet dissolved. Even in the intermittent streetlight she could see the way his lashes were sweeping down over his eyes, and the equally telltale glint of gold in their depths. All her questions—unformed, unshaped, unspoken—vanished from her head. All there was in her consciousness was the knowledge that she was as eager as he was to get back to his apartment, be swept into his arms and into his bed. To experience the ecstasy that awaited her there.

The most blissful place in the world to be…

Connie was chopping vegetables again, and this time she was not interrupted by Dante. Instead, he was overseeing her progress through the latest recipe she was happily trying out, reading the instructions to her in instant translation.

Happiness filled her. This undemanding, unglamorous domestic scene was dearer to her than all the indulgent luxury of shopping for designer clothes, even though that came with her still incredulous delight at seeing admiration for her transformed appearance in Dante's eyes. It was dearer to her than all the pleasurable excitement of him taking her sightseeing, speeding them away in his scarily fast supercar, which he obviously got a boyish kick out of driving, to while away the hours exploring the lushly scenic countryside, soaking up the atmosphere of the historic towns and medieval cities with which Italy was so richly endowed.

Just doing something as simple, as easy-going, as chopping vegetables, with Dante reading her a recipe, made her feel supremely satisfied.

It's all I want—just to be with him. I don't need anything more. I don't need designer clothes, or lavish sightseeing, wonderful though all that is. All I want is…Dante.

At some point she must go back to thinking about a career of some sort—or she might be able to do a

Master's out here in Italy, for all she knew, or perhaps even teach English Literature to Italian students? It was all to find out…all to discover. But there was no rush, no urgency. For now she was content—oh, *so* content—simply to be here with Dante like this.

Her eyes went to him now, absorbed in flicking lazily through some other enticing recipes on the website, leaning against the breakfast bar, his free hand casually curved around a beer glass from which he drank from time to time. A lock of stray hair had fallen over his brow, and his sculpted cheekbones caught the light from one of the kitchen's ceiling spots. He'd changed out of his business suit, and the soft cashmere of his sweater lovingly moulded his torso…casual chinos emphasised the length of his legs.

Her breath caught—how fabulous he looked, and how wonderful it was just to stand here and look at him and know that she was with him.

That wave of emotion came again…sweeter and more powerful. She knew it for what it was. Knew it and gloried in it. Gave herself over to it completely.

It was the most precious emotion of all…

Dante glanced up from the screen. 'OK, so now add the chopped tomatoes to the mix. Then you need to slice and salt the aubergines to draw off the excess liquid and add them too. Because they'll be salty you don't need to add any more salt, the recipe says.'

'Yes, Chef,' said Connie dutifully, with a nod and a smile.

His answering smile was a slash of white. 'Tomorrow night I'll be cooking and you can be the one giving orders,' he said, and laughed.

They ate at the apartment every night—sometimes cooking themselves, sometimes ordering in. At weekends they went touring, staying in boutique hotels full of charm and character, though always very upmarket. They ate out then, of course—both lunch and dinner.

But they hadn't been out to dine in Milan since that evening with Rafaello, some weeks ago now. Connie had no objections—she loved these domesticated evenings with Dante, just her and him in his apartment. There would be plenty of time to meet his friends here in Milan, go out in public with him as she had when they saw Raf. For now, she was happy—more than happy—to devote herself to him. Just the two of them, together.

Like an old married couple...

It was another happy thought.

A contented smile hovered at her lips as she reached for the salt to sprinkle it on the sliced aubergine on the chopping board. The herby aroma of the already cooking vegetables was enticing, and she was looking forward to the meal. Dante had poured her a glass of white wine, fresh and crisp, as an *aperitivo*, and she reached for it now, taking a sip of its chilled fruitiness.

'OK, I've found a recipe for my turn tomorrow,' Dante announced, and described it to her. 'I'll bookmark it, so if you like maybe you can pick the ingredients up tomorrow?'

'Happy to.' Connie smiled. She was getting used to shopping for groceries, trying out her halting phrase-book Italian.

I need to knuckle down and really learn the language properly, she thought in passing, crossing to the sink to rinse the excess salt off the aubergines.

Her vocabulary was improving every day, but her grammar was very shaky, she knew. And to settle fully into a new country one really did need to crack the language.

Adding the final ingredient to the pot, and turning down the heat to let it simmer till it was ready, she picked up her wine glass and went to join Dante at the bar, perched on a high stools. A memory came to her of how she'd done just that at the swish cocktail bar in London, when Dante had seen her for the very first time since her makeover. How his stunned gaze had devoured her.

It had changed everything he'd ever thought about her.

Changed everything between them from that night onwards to this moment now.

That same wave of emotion went through her, just as before, and as before she gave herself over to it, so dearly precious it was to her.

'Saluti,' Dante said casually, clicking his beer glass against her wine glass and sliding his tablet aside. 'So,' he asked, 'where do you fancy going this weekend?'

'What about the mountains?' Connie suggested. 'The Italian Alps? Or are they too far away?'

'Not at all,' Dante assured her, and ran through some of the options.

They went on discussing an itinerary for the weekend and then, dinner ready, repaired to the dining area of the spacious apartment. It was a long and lazy meal, followed by a long and lazy lounge on the sofa, where Connie happily indulged Dante's desire to watch a football match on the huge wall-mounted screen. She was content to curl up against him, reading a woman's magazine in Italian—or attempting to read it—interrupting him from time to time to ask for translations of words she didn't yet know.

'You're getting pretty good.' Dante dropped an admiring kiss on her head.

'Well, I need to study the language properly,' Connie said. 'I'd love to get really fluent.'

'Is that necessary?' Dante asked. 'Considering—'

He broke off, his attention suddenly snapping back to the screen as the commentator's voice rose in excitement and the crowd became even noisier. A goal was scored, and Dante enthusiastically punched the air with a happy exclamation.

The match ended soon after, with the team Dante supported winning, much to his satisfaction. He reached for his coffee, draining it down.

'By the way, I've got some business coming up that will take me down to Rome—at the end of next week, most likely. We could add the weekend and see the Eternal City in all its glory, if you like?'

Connie smiled. 'Oh, that would be brilliant!' she said. A thought struck her. 'Would you want to meet up with Rafaello?' She frowned a moment. 'Is he part-nered, by the way? I mean, I know he's not married—he doesn't wear a ring. Not that that necessarily means anything, of course,' she said, conscious that Dante did not either. Nor did she.

Maybe now we should?

The thought was in her head before she could stop it. But Dante was speaking, banishing it as swiftly as it came.

'Raf,' he said, his voice dry, 'is what I believe in English is called "a smooth operator". Getting him to the altar, or anywhere close, will take a very clever female indeed...'

Connie frowned. 'Maybe he'll just find he's fallen in love one day, with the woman he wants to spend the rest of his life with.'

Dante didn't answer, and she twisted her head slightly to glance up at him. The veiled look was back in his eyes. Then he gave a shrug.

'That's a very romantic view of life,' he said.

There was a definite edge in his voice. Connie could hear it.

'Raf's far too cynical to believe in love. He's a born lawyer.'

Then his expression changed, with the veiled look disappearing and a far more open one taking its place—one Connie was all too familiar with.

He dropped a soft, sensual kiss on her upturned lips. 'Why the hell are we discussing Raf?' he said in mock indignation, kissing her again.

His kiss deepened, and Connie felt herself melting

into it, as she always did when he kissed her like this. In moments all thoughts of Rafaello, all thoughts of anything at all, were lost—and so was Connie, drowning in the sweet sensuality of Dante's kisses…

CHAPTER SEVEN

DANTE DEPRESSED THE ACCELERATOR, speeding up along the autostrada. They were closing in on Rome and would be there in time for dinner. Beside him, Connie was gazing with interest at the passing landscape, as she had all the way from Milan.

'There's *so* much to learn about Italy!' she exclaimed. 'I just want to gulp it all down now that I'm living here.'

Dante made no answer, focusing on overtaking a lorry irritatingly in the way of his powerful, fast, low-slung car. But Connie's words echoed in his mind. Hung there a moment.

Then she was asking him another question, about a town the exit to which they had just passed, and he gave her the best answer he could, glad of the distraction. He was not entirely comfortable about why he'd been glad of it, but he put it out of his mind. He was looking forward to Rome. Looking forward to squeezing a few days away from the business clients he was seeing while he was there and showing the city off to Connie. They'd meet up with Rafaello one evening, but that was all.

And if Raf damn well tries any of his tricks—oh-so-amusing to him but to no one else, like he did with Bianca in Milan—he can take a hike!

He glanced at Connie, his expression softening as it always did when he looked at her. She'd enjoy Rome, he'd make sure of that, for he always wanted to please her. And in turn she was so appreciative—as sweet-natured as she had always been.

He knew and rejoiced in the fact that she was finally without the cares and worries that had assailed her while she was looking after her grandmother, even though their marriage had eased the financial pressure on her. Now there were no pressures on her at all, and he could ensure that she was enjoying herself as she so richly deserved.

And he could share in that enjoyment. He was enjoying all they did together, whether it was sightseeing or having quiet evenings in Milan, cooking dinner together, vegging on the sofa, watching undemanding TV and then heading off to bed, with her as eager as he was to reach their final destination of the day.

Has it ever been like this for me before?

It was an unnecessary question. He knew it hadn't been. And it was all thanks to Connie.

She's so easy to be with—happy, good-tempered, sweet-natured... And as passionate in making love with me as any man could dream of. She gives herself completely...

And he, in return, did all he could to show her how much he desired her in return.

His thoughts turned to how quickly she could arouse and inflame and then satiate him...

'Where are we going to be staying in Rome? Remind me again?'

Connie's question interrupted thoughts that were getting too heated for a long car journey, and he was a little relieved.

'The Falcone,' he answered, overtaking another lorry that was going as slowly as a slug, relishing the acceleration of his powerful car at his command. 'It's a little out of the *centro storico*, but quieter for that reason. Just a taxi ride from all the sights in Rome. Speaking of which—what's top of your agenda to visit once I'm clear of my business appointments?'

'Ooh, there's so much to choose from!' she answered.

They ran through some of the major attractions, drawing up a flexible list, and continued to discuss them that evening over dinner at their hotel.

The Falcone, converted from a grand nineteenth-century villa, was set on the slope of one of Rome's fabled hills, surrounded by extensive gardens and with a view over the city. There was a pool in the grounds, and Connie had assured Dante that she would be more than happy to spend her first day enjoying it and the hotel's amenities in the still-warm weather of early autumn, while he went off to his business meetings.

He would be glad when he was done with his appointments, though, he thought again. And was looking forward to spending a leisurely few days here with Connie.

It was a quite different pace of life from the one he'd had to keep when his grandfather had been alive. He'd been at his beck and call, always focused on business, snatching brief, shallow affairs when he could fit one into his non-stop schedule. Now his time was his own, and if he wanted to cut back on his working hours—well, he was free to do so. And not constrained to brief affairs any longer, either.

He shied his thoughts away. He didn't want to dwell on the restrictions of his past. He just wanted to enjoy the present—the entirely pleasurable present. It was enough. More than enough.

Bidding Connie farewell as she packed a bag for the pool, he headed off. A hotel car would take him into the city for the first of his appointments, and then he was taking a client to lunch, followed by another two meetings in the afternoon. He was cramming them all into one day, so as to devote himself to Connie's entertainment thereafter.

He was looking forward not just to being with her—that was always good—but to seeing the sights again himself. His visits to Rome, as to any other city, had always been work-focused. Now, with Connie, he could take a more relaxed approach.

He'd just bade farewell to his lunchtime companion, after a mutually satisfactory discussion, when he was hailed by a familiar if unexpected voice.

'Raf? What are you doing here?' Dante glanced up

from checking the bill for the meal—a hefty sum, but worth it for the valuable client he had just impressed with his financial recommendations.

'Same as you—I've been lunching with a client.' He sat himself down at Dante's table. 'So, what evening would be good for us to meet up? Given the Falcone's renowned gourmet chef, I'd be happy to come to you.' He paused, glancing at Dante. Then, 'How's Connie?' he asked.

'Fine,' said Dante. 'I'm showing her Rome. The Forum tomorrow, and the Hippodrome too, and then St Peter's and the Vatican the day after.'

Rafaello leant back in his chair. 'I'm giving a party at the weekend—it's my birthday, in case you'd forgotten. Why not come along?'

Dante shook his head. 'No, I don't think so—thanks all the same.'

Rafaello raised his eyebrows. 'Why not? You'll know enough people there through me, and Connie would enjoy it, I think.' He let his eyes rest on Dante in a way Dante did not care for. 'And I'm sure people would like to meet your wife.'

Dante felt his face set. 'Connie would find it overwhelming,' he said tersely. 'I wouldn't expose her to all that!'

'Expose her—or you?'

Dante's expression hardened, and he spoke bluntly, knowing he needed to make himself clear. 'Raf, back off. I know you find it amusing—hilarious, even—that I had to marry to get hold of my inheritance, but it's been a sore point with me ever since. Both your amusement *and* the fact that my hand was forced from beyond the grave!'

His friend held up his hand, as if to acknowledge Dante's objection. But the look in his eye continued to be speculative.

'What?' Dante demanded. His irritation was rising, and he didn't want Raf needling him.

But Rafaello only looked at him inscrutably.

His damn lawyer's face, Dante thought, irritation spiking again.

'Nothing at all,' Rafaello said smoothly. He rose to his feet, with the same unreadable expression on his face. 'OK, forget my party—but why don't I come over to the Falcone for dinner? Say tomorrow night? How would that be?'

Dante agreed with a rather terse, 'Fine, yes.'

But as Rafaello strolled off he was still conscious of that feeling of irritation. Annoyance. It was none of Raf's damn business, him and Connie. They were fine as they were—just fine.

Just leave us alone—that's what we want.

As if on cue, his phone pinged—it was a text from her.

Hope your business lunch went OK. I'm lounging by the pool. Dead lazy!

On impulse, he texted back.

If you want a change of scene, how about meeting me for cocktails later, when my afternoon appointments are done? We could do the Spanish Steps and the Trevi Fountain if that appeals?

Her reply was enthusiastic, and he was pleased. He felt his irritation at Raf dissipating. Raf just didn't get what he and Connie were about, that was all.

In a much better mood, he headed off for his next appointment, checking out a good venue for cocktails as he did so. There were plenty to choose from…

When Connie met him later, near the foot of the famous Spanish Steps, he guided her to a bar where they could sit outside and watch the Romans—and the tourists—making their evening *passeggiata.* Then, having made the ritual ascent and descent of the steps themselves, he took her for dinner.

Afterwards they ended up at the Trevi Fountain, floodlit for the evening, its water luminescent. It was still jammed with tourists.

'Ready to throw your coin in the fountain?' Dante smiled down at Connie as they edged their way forward.

'Do I need to?' she asked.

'Only if you want to be sure of coming back to Rome again,' Dante teased.

'What? Even if it's only coming from Milan? I thought the legend was just for those living in other countries? Oh, well, I'd better be on the safe side, I guess!'

She dug out a coin, turned her back on the glories of Bernini's masterpiece waterworks, and threw it over her shoulder in time-honoured fashion. She looked round to see where it had landed, but it was impossible to tell amongst all the coins under the water.

'They get collected daily and given to charity,' Dante assured her. 'Come on—we'd better get out of here before we get pushed into the fountain by the crowd. Let's get a *gelato*.' He indicated the famous *gelataria* to one side of the fountain. 'And then a coffee before heading back to the hotel.'

He put his arm around her shoulders as they strolled away from the fountain. As ever, it felt good to have her at his side.

Choosing a *gelato* from the huge selection on offer took some time, and then, choices made, they wandered off into the still-mild night. It was relaxed and companionable, walking with her arm in arm, consuming their ice-creams, eying up likely cafés for their late-night coffee.

He told her that he'd run into Raf that day, agreed to dinner at their hotel the following night, and then he trailed another suggestion, putting it to her as they sat down at a pavement café and ordered their coffee.

'Once you've seen enough of Rome, how about we keep heading south and take in Amalfi as well?' he asked.

She raised her eyebrows. 'That's quite a distance. Can you afford to take so much time off work? I'm more than happy, truly, to head back to Milan.'

Her expression changed, and he saw there was a tinge of anxiety in it.

'Dante, honestly…you don't have to show me all of Italy in one go. There's loads of time for me to see it, little by little.'

She took his hand, squeezed it as if reassuring him.

'I'm perfectly happy in Milan, I promise.'

He cocked an eyebrow 'You're not that keen on my apartment, though, are you?' he said perceptively. 'It's too modern for you.' He smiled knowingly.

'Well, it's ideal for city living,' she allowed. 'But with the countryside of Lombardy being so beautiful, it's a shame for you not to have at least a weekend place there to get away to, out of the city.' She frowned a moment. 'Where were you brought up, Dante? Where did your grandfather live?'

He answered her, but unwillingly, not wanting to dwell on the past. The present was what he was enjoying—and he liked it that way.

'He had a massive mansion on the outskirts of the city. I sold it when I inherited. It cost a fortune to run. It wasn't ancestral, or anything like that—he bought it when he first made serious money. I never liked it much,' he admitted. 'One of the few things I had in common with my father,' he heard himself adding.

Connie was silent for a moment. 'That's a shame,' she said quietly. 'Were…were you and he not close before he was killed so tragically?'

'No,' said Dante.

He reached for his coffee. He didn't want to spell out his life story for Connie. There was no point.

He looked across at her, his face shuttered. 'I've told you, Connie. I was brought up by my grandfather.

My parents were off, gadding about, social butterflies the pair of them. My grandfather worked me hard, but I grew up with a sense of responsibility and the expectation of being the one to run Cavelli Finance after my grandfather died. He was fond of me, in his own way, but he was a tough cookie—he'd made his fortune from scratch, and that requires a certain level of ruthlessness. As he aged, he got keen on my taking over more and more, being trained up for the job, but always under his close supervision—supervision that extended to way beyond work.'

As he went on he heard his voice change and tighten.

'He wanted to supervise my whole life. Make sure I lived it the way he thought best.' His gaze slipped away. 'Maybe as he got older it made him think of posterity…the next generation…that sort of thing. And maybe,' he said, still not looking at her, 'that's why he tried to manipulate me with his will. Forcing me to marry. Presumably he thought to kickstart the next generation after me.'

His gaze snapped back to her. Sharp now with remembered anger.

'I was furious at being manipulated from beyond the grave. Determined to find a way to outwit him— outmanoeuvre him.' His expression lightened finally. 'And I did. I found *you*, Connie. And together—well, together we've found a solution to our own problems, and it's worked out well. I think we'd both agree on that…' His expression changed again, his eyes glinting, voice softening. 'And we've both got a bonus payoff neither of us dreamt of at the start of all this.'

He reached for her hand, lying inert beside her coffee cup, and raised it to his lips, kissing her knuckles softly, sensuously.

'An incredible bonus…' he said huskily.

Abruptly, he let her hand go, bolting down the rest of his coffee, finding his wallet and tossing the requisite notes on the table.

Holding out his hand to Connie, he got to his feet. 'Shall we get back to the hotel?' he suggested.

Desire was unhidden in his voice.

Connie gave a sigh of deep contentment, looking around the small, cobbled *piazza* lined with ancient-looking higgledy-piggledy houses, some draped with ivy, some with peeling paint. The whole place had, to her mind, a charming, boho feel to it.

After taking in the splendours of St Peter's, she'd asked to see the Trastevere area across the Tiber, and Dante had obliged, after warning her that it had become very touristy, and could be down at heel in places. But Connie liked it, despite his warning, and said as much now, as they settled down to have a late lunch at a very ordinary-looking *trattoria* whose simple, pasta-dominated menu was a far cry from the gourmet delicacies conjured up by the Falcone's celebrity chef.

Her spaghetti, when it arrived, was delicious, and even Dante conceded his was as well, and washed it down with one of the many craft beers for which, he told her, Trastevere was famous.

He glanced around him. 'God knows when I was last here,' he remarked. 'Probably when I was a student, with a bunch of mates, enjoying the bars… sampling all the beers! It gets very lively in the evenings, and that would have suited me at the time. Not that I ever got much time to gallivant about,' he added, forking up his pasta, his voice changing. 'My grandfather kept me on a tight rein.'

Connie looked at him with sympathy. From this and what he'd mentioned to her over coffee the night before, it sounded as if his grandfather hadn't been easy to live with.

'Were you at university here in Rome?' she asked.

He shook his head. 'No, Milan—and I had to live at home for the duration. I managed to go AWOL sometimes, though…heading down here to Rome, where Raf was studying, and I experienced a bit of nightlife then.'

Connie's expression was troubled. 'That seems pretty harsh of your grandfather,' she said. Her voice softened. 'My gran urged me to choose a uni far from the West Country. She wanted me to be independent. Quite the opposite from your grandfather's attitude,' she said, with sympathy in her voice.

Dante shrugged. 'He didn't want me getting a taste for self-indulgence, like my father had.'

She shook her head. 'Everyone needs to enjoy their student years, as well as studying hard.'

He reached for his beer, took a slug. 'Well, like

I said, I was kept on a tight leash. Which is why I was so determined to break it after his death. And to keep it broken.'

He set his glass down with a decided click and she could see the tension in him. Her gaze was troubled. Dante might have been raised without any money worries at all, but that didn't mean he'd had an easy time of it.

But that's all over now. Now he's free from his grandfather's controlling nature. Free to make his own choices in life.

Wasn't he?

The answer was instant.

Yes—yes, he is. And he's chosen me.

After all, why else would she be here with him now?

And he's happy now. I know he is! Anyone can see that—anyone at all.

She felt her spirits lift and that precious emotion that she hugged so close welling through her, washing towards him, embracing him.

He'll be happy from now on, too. I'll make sure of it.

His eyes met hers across the table and she saw them soften.

'So, what shall we do after lunch?' he asked, his voice holding the cheerful warmth it usually had.

She was glad of it. Glad to respond in kind.

Getting stuck into her spaghetti again, as he was too, she ran over some of the attractions she'd read about in Trastevere.

'There's the old ghetto area, and the Basilica di Santa Maria, which my guidebook says has mosaics by Cavallini—of whom, I admit freely, I have never previously heard, but which look beautiful in the photos. Or we could go to the Galleria Corsini,' she ran on enthusiastically. 'Which is, apparently, a baroque palace with paintings by Titian and Caravaggio, of whom I definitely *have* heard!' She looked at Dante a little anxiously. 'But if you're bored we don't have to,' she assured him.

'Let's see everything while we're here,' he answered cheerfully.

The shuttered look, and the long shadows cast by the past, had all gone from his face, reassuring Connie.

'Then we can get back to the hotel in time for a late dip in the pool, before we primp ourselves for Mr Uber-Smooth Rafaello,' he said sardonically.

Connie had laughed, but all the same, by the time she was ready to head down to the hotel's bar to meet up with Rafaello that evening, she knew she had indeed primped herself for the occasion.

The old-gold-coloured dress she'd chosen came with a matching hip-length jacket, loose-fitting and elegant, with a beautiful soft sheen to it, and she wore her hair up, painstakingly pinned to give her a little height and a touch of what she hoped was sophistication.

The overall effect certainly drew Dante's praise and admiration, and she basked in its warmth.

As they went into the elegant bar area adjoining the restaurant she saw Rafaello had already arrived, and he got to his feet, paying her an extravagant compliment and smiling down at her.

It was set to be a convivial evening. The gourmet menu on offer was superb, the vintage wines equally so, and Rafaello was on form—and openly amused by Connie saying they'd spent the day in Trastevere.

'Trastevere?' A musing look came into Rafaello's face. 'I seem to recall Dante and I and some fellow *raggazzi* spent a pretty wild night there once in our misspent youth!'

He spoke lightly, but Connie replied with a troubled look in her eyes. 'Dante told me—but he didn't really have a chance to have much of a misspent youth, did he? Thanks to his grandfather.'

'Oh, he fitted in some misspending for all that— as the likes of the fiery Bianca can testify,' Rafaello observed, with that sardonic note in his voice again. 'Mind you...' He took a reflective mouthful of wine, his eyes resting on both Connie and Dante for a moment. 'It looks like all that's changed now.'

Connie saw Dante's face alter. Close down. Like it had briefly when they'd had lunch and he'd talked about his grandfather's strictures. Clearly he didn't like Rafaello talking about all the exes Dante had in his past. She was glad of it.

'So, what are your plans after Rome?' Rafaello asked, changing the subject briskly. 'Are you heading back to Milan? And what about after that? Are you happy with Dante's bachelor pad apartment, Connie, or do you want to go house-hunting with him? Somewhere more settled for you, perhaps? More suitable for connubial domestic bliss?'

He'd spoken lightly, in nothing more than pleasant enquiry, but Dante set down his knife and fork and looked straight across at his friend. Connie could see that the shuttered look was still on his face, and his eyes were glinting—not in a good way.

'Raf, I have told you before,' he spelt out. 'Back off. I am aware of your deep amusement over my having to marry as I did, but that joke has been played out! Now…' his voice took on a warning note, became admonitory and deadly serious '…just lay off.'

Connie felt a stab or alarm, but his expression changed again and he threw a glance at her and she could see concern in it—and reassurance.

'Please do not involve Connie in your amusement. She has been an absolute Trojan in all of this. I can't thank her enough for what she's done for me, coming to my rescue the way she did. Yes, I hope I have made things a great deal easier for her, too, financially, but now…' he reached out, brushed Connie's arm, his voice softening '…after all she did for her grandmother she deserves this break—and I'm glad she is having it. A good, long, luxurious holiday, as much time as I can give her and a whole lot of pampering. That is what she totally deserves!'

Dante cast a warm look at her—yet for some reason this time it did not warm her.

His gaze snapped back to Rafaello. 'I won't have Connie upset or embarrassed. *Por Dio!* She's coped really well with a difficult and insanely awkward situation and she can do without your unfunny jibes. And so,' he said pointedly, 'can I. Not to mention that I can *definitely* do without your trying to make trouble with—'

He broke off, switched to Italian, speaking rapidly. It was too fast for Connie to follow, but she caught words here and there—and a name. She dropped her eyes away—not wanting to be the cause, however unintentionally, of any discord between the two friends.

As Dante finished Rafaello said something, short and to the point, it seemed. She glanced up, seeing Dante scowl, his mouth compressed. Then, in a deliberate gesture, he reached for his wine. Reverted to English.

'OK—let's drop the subject.'

His tone of voice had relaxed, and Connie could hear him trying to inject good humour into it.

'You asked what our plans were after Rome?' he said, addressing Rafaello. 'I'm thinking of taking Connie down the Amalfi coast. I know it's getting late in the year, but this run of fine weather is tempting me to risk it. What do you think, Connie?' Dante turned his head to her, an enquiring look in his eyes.

'Well, it would be lovely, but...' She let her voice trail off. Emotions were rising in her and words were failing her. Her Italian was rudimentary, still, and highly imperfect. Had she really heard Dante say what she thought he had? Why would he say it? She must have misunderstood...

Mustn't she?

Rafaello took over smoothly. Although Connie was aware that he was observing her from beneath lowered eyebrows.

'But she's terrified of the thought of your driving along those hairpin bends,' he said lightly.

Connie gave a flickering smile. 'Dante does like to drive fast,' she conceded. 'But I'm getting used to it,' she added quietly.

'I won't crash, and that's a promise,' Dante said, patting her arm reassuringly.

As reassuringly as when he'd praised her for agreeing to marry him so he could inherit his grandfather's fortune and for putting up with their bizarre marriage…

She used her uncertain smile again—all she could manage right now. She was aware that something seemed to be making a lump in her throat…or maybe it was in her stomach. She wasn't sure. She only knew she had to go on conversing as convivially as Dante and Rafaello were now doing again. Because for some reason it was essential she did so.

Their gourmet meal continued, but though she knew she was eating the most delicious and terrifyingly expensive dishes, she knew she was not doing them justice. And not because of all the calories she'd cut down on, but for a reason she did not want to think about.

Must not think about.

Not now.

Not yet.

But she did feel, for all that, as if she were a bal-

loon which had just been punctured with a tiny pin-
prick, deflating very slowly…

Worse, she was aware that Rafaello, despite his
bonhomie, seemed to be keeping her under surveil-
lance through those lidded eyes of his. As if he were in
lawyer mode, assessing a witness…or a defendant…

A defendant with something to hide…

It made her overreact, to hide her feelings, and she
became more outwardly cheerful, more vocal, trying to participate in the lively conversation, focusing
on Dante's proposed expedition to Amalfi and what
awaited her there.

'I'm not sure I can face Pompeii, though,' Connie
heard herself saying. 'So unbearably sad. All those
lives destroyed…'

There was a melancholy note in her voice, and yet
she knew it was not just because of the hideous tragedy of two millennia ago, sweeping over the unsus-
pecting Pompeiians. It was about something much
closer…far more personal.

Something that she did not want to give voice to.
Could not bear to contemplate right now.

'Then we shan't go,' Dante said decisively. 'I'm
not having you upset. But how about a trip across to
Capri instead? If the weather is good enough?'

'Oh, that sounds much nicer,' she said gratefully.

Dante gave her another warm smile, personal and
intimate—and, again, it should have reassured her.
But something was happening to her…something she
couldn't explain and wasn't sure about. Despite her
chattiness she felt distracted—and disquieted by the

feeling that Rafaello was watching her, speculating about her…

Does he think I'm bad for Dante? Clingy…? Possessive, maybe?

It was an unpleasant thought. He'd never approved of Dante's marriage from the first—she knew that.

She became anxious for the meal to finish, for reasons she couldn't articulate, but when it finally did, in leisurely fashion, and Rafaello took his leave, lightly kissing Connie on the cheek and slapping Dante equally lightly on his shoulder as he thanked him for his hospitality, adjuring both of them to enjoy the rest of their stay in Rome and then Amalfi, Connie found she still wasn't relaxing.

Dante took her hand as they made their way towards the lifts, having waved off Rafaello in the hotel lobby.

'Let's have another coffee and a nightcap upstairs,' he said genially.

Connie smiled and nodded, conscious of feeling constricted. Up in their room, with its view over the city of Rome, and the vast dome of St Peter's lit up, Dante flicked on the in-room coffee machine and poured them both a liqueur—sweet for her, strong for him—carrying them over to the sofa positioned by the window.

'Too cold for the balcony,' he said, and Connie agreed.

He sat down beside her, stretching out his legs and putting his arm companionably around her shoulder.

Then he kicked off his shoes and flexed his ankles, loosening his tie with his free hand.

Connie glanced at him. There was something about a loosened tie that made her insides melt, and combined with the incipient signs of darkening along Dante's jaw she felt the melting accelerate. Oh, sweet heaven, he was just so irresistible…

For the first time since Dante had silenced Rafaello she felt her feelings of disquiet subside. She nestled into Dante's encircling arm, reaching for her liqueur and taking a tiny sip of its sweet but fiery contents. She could hear the coffee machine beginning to perk as Dante reached for his own glass.

'Good old Raf,' he remarked, and his voice was much more relaxed, Connie was glad to hear. 'Always knows how to push my buttons… But I don't want him doing the same to you.' He took a taste of his liqueur. 'I can take it—and I give back as good as he hands out—but I don't want you dragged into it. He doesn't mean anything by it, but all the same…'

His expression darkened, and annoyance was now visible in it.

'His warped sense humour did enough damage that night in Milan. I told him straight off that I'd had to go into damage limitation mode with Bianca Delamondi, and phone her the next day to tell her he was just fooling around.'

Connie swallowed. She'd hoped she hadn't understood the gist of what Dante had said to Rafaello in Italian over dinner earlier. But now…

'Dante, is that what you said to Rafaello tonight?

I… I caught some words, but I wasn't sure I was understanding. Did you say you'd told Bianca that of course we weren't married…'

Dante pulled back from her a fraction, to look at her upturned face. 'It was the easiest way to get her off my case,' he said warily.

Connie stared. 'But…but we *are* married,' she said.

Dante lifted a hand, then dropped it. 'That's our business—and no one else's. I'm not going to tell the world what I was forced into doing. The only person who knows other than my grandfather's lawyers is Raf. And I want to keep it that way,' he said tightly.

There was irritation in his voice, in his face. More than that—a taut sense of frustration. Resistance. Resentment.

Rejection of what he's been forced into.

A word formed in her brain. Brutal and stark.

Denial.

She felt cold to the bone, but Dante was still speaking.

'That's why I've kept you to myself,' he said. 'I don't want any talk or speculation—let alone having to make explanations. Like I've said, it's no one else's business!'

His expression softened, but the cold was still running in her veins. He dropped a light kiss on her upswept hair, then relaxed back again. He was cradling his brandy glass in his cupped free hand. The other was warm on her shoulder as she sat nestled against him. But the warmth of his hand did not penetrate the coldness filling her.

Nor did the words he spoke now, his voice becoming ruminative.

'The thing is, you and I have had to cope with a situation that neither of us would have given the time of day even to consider in normal circumstances. But we were forced into it. If I could have got my inheritance any other way, I would have. And if you could have protected your grandmother any other way, you would have. Neither of us *wanted* this marriage, and the consequences have been a challenge for us both in different ways.'

His voice softened, warmed. Yet there was no trace of warmth in her.

'You've been a godsend to me, Connie. You know that. And I hope you know just how much I appreciate what you did for me, agreeing to my proposition. I meant what I said—that after everything you've been through, caring for your grandmother, you deserve to have a wonderful time now.'

He dropped another light kiss on her hair, and then crooked his head forward to reach her cheek, brushing it with gentle affection. His eyes met hers, and in them she could see what had always before set her melting.

But now—now everything seemed frozen. As if a glaze of ice had formed over him—and her. Chilling her to the core.

'And you don't need me to tell you how fantastic this time with you has been,' he said gruffly.

He took another slow mouthful of his brandy, drawing a little away from her so he could see her more clearly.

His eyes held hers. 'I want you to know that, despite Raf's idiotic remarks, I completely respect that you have your own life to lead and that you want to make a career for yourself—whether in publishing or academia or anything else you choose. We still have another good few months of our marriage to run before I can safely avoid any legal challenge by my grandfather's lawyers, but you absolutely must not feel under any obligation whatsoever to stay in Italy with me till then. Whenever you want to head back to the UK, just say the word.'

He brushed her lips with his, and Connie could taste the heat of the brandy on them—a heat that was in his eyes as well. Which was strange, because her lips felt frozen, just like the rest of her.

'Of course I'm self-indulgent enough to hope that won't be too soon. Let's definitely pack Amalfi in!' A thought clearly struck him. 'And with winter heading our way, how would you feel about checking out the Dolomites? Have you ever been skiing?'

Connie swallowed. 'No…never…' she said. She managed to get the words out through stiff lips, but she didn't know how.

Dante smiled in satisfaction. 'Then why not give it a go? The Dolomites are spectacular in their own right. We could have Christmas there, maybe. What do you say to that?'

She didn't answer. Couldn't. Could only give the

briefest of flickering smiles and clutch her liqueur glass in fingers that were suddenly numb.

Like her insides…

Dante was still talking. 'The best snow is after the New Year, mind you. And maybe after Christmas we'd like a taste of heat again—to head for warmer climes. The Seychelles, Mauritius, the Maldives… Loads to choose from. And plenty of time in the next four months or so to do it before we need to think about our divorce.'

She heard him speaking, but his voice seemed to be coming from very far away, across a gulf that had without warning opened up like a chasm between them. A gaping, jagged chasm into which she was falling, falling, falling…

And she could do nothing at all to stop it.

CHAPTER EIGHT

THE PALMS OF Connie's hands were moving slowly, sensuously, across the planed smooth torso of Dante's chest, the tips of her fingers tracing every contour of his perfect, honed musculature. Her head dipped to let her lips follow the path of her fingers. She heard Dante groan dimly from the pleasure she was giving him.

She was making love to him. Making love to him with all the dedication and all the devotion that filled her.

As if it might be the very last time she would ever make love to him…

Slowly, she moved her naked body over his, her lips caressing the strong column of his throat, to seek and find what she yearned for. The answering softness of his mouth as it yielded, with another low groan in his throat, to her kisses.

She felt his hands come around her waist, guiding her over him as her breasts made contact with his chest, pressing her down on him as her thighs slid across his. Another groan broke from him and she could feel his arousal strengthen. It called to her own arousal, and she felt her breath quicken, her pulse quicken, her longing for him overwhelming her.

Their kisses deepened, their mouths opening to each other as his hands tightened around her waist. She moved her hips slowly, sensually, knowing she was increasing his arousal, loving how strong he was, how fully engorged. She felt her own body answer in kind, the delicate tissues of her femininity moistening. Instinctively, she parted her thighs, slackening them, positioning herself over him, lifting just a little to catch him and guide him into her waiting, aching body.

His moan matched hers and her hands splayed either side of his head, her back arching to take him, oh, so fully into her. Her need for him was absolute, and only with him was her completion possible.

She moved over him rhythmically and his thighs, so taut and hard beneath hers, strained as he thrust himself up into her. His hands were like a vice around her waist now, splayed out over the roundness of her hips, holding her to him exactly where he wanted her to be, needed her to be—where she needed to be, ached to be. The only place in all the world.

Her body fused with his, taking him as she gave herself, as her arousal intensified, matching him movement for movement, knowing that the release that would soon come for him and for her would be…

Glorious.

A radiance of sensation that was so intense it was unbearable blossomed inside her and she cried out, her head falling back, her hair streaming down her back as her body surged with his, melting, dissolving into ecstasy.

She was his!

Oh, she was his he was hers.

They were one—one flesh, one union, one body, one pulsing, beating heart…

She dropped to him, a sob breaking from her, hands clutching him, holding him closer and yet closer still. She could still feel him throbbing inside her as the waves of her own body continued to pulse gently, holding him tightly inside her.

Slowly, so very, very slowly, the passion ebbed from them both, slackening their bodies, leaving them fulfilled and completed. Their closeness now was the closeness of limbs suddenly heavy and torpid, exhaustion fusing them one to the other. Her hands slipped to his arms, curving around his biceps, and her cheek rested on his shoulder.

She felt his hands slide down to rest on her flanks. His mouth grazed her lowered brow so lightly, his voice, low and drowsy, murmured her name. And then, her eyelids heavy…so heavy…sweet, embracing sleep drew her down into its consoling peace.

Dante heard his phone bleep and reached for it. Who the hell was calling him at this time of night, when all he wanted to do, in his sated post-coital state, was sleep through till morning?

When he saw the caller ID he groaned, but accepted the call, levering himself out of bed and padding across to the far side of the room so as not to disturb Connie. The conversation was blessedly brief, but the outcome far from welcome.

Swiftly, and deeply reluctantly, he set a low-volume alarm on his phone and headed back to bed, enfolding Connie in his arms. It was the place he liked her to be, with her soft body embraced by his.

Sleep swept over him again until, still at an ungodly early hour, his alarm went off. It didn't wake Connie, and he was glad as he levered himself totally unwillingly from their bed and went into the en suite bathroom for as swift a shower and shave as he could manage.

Quickly dressed, he crossed back to the bed and Connie's sleeping form. For a few precious seconds he gazed down at her in the soft light thrown from the bathroom.

How truly beautiful she was! Every time he looked at her he wondered at how she'd concealed such loveliness from him for so long. He loved everything about her—from the way her hair curled over her rounded shoulder to the way her eyelashes dusted her soft cheeks…the way her lips, slightly parted as she breathed steadily in slumber, were tempting him even now to brush a kiss upon their velvet contours.

But, damn it, just when she looked so alluring—so embraceable—just when he'd been looking forward to another lotus-eating day with her, relaxed and leisurely, wandering around Rome, now he was going to have to do without her.

Accidenti.

He let his mouth touch hers, just for the briefest moment, and then he lifted away, gently rocking her shoulder as he did.

Her eyes fluttered open, fastening to his. For a second he saw something flare in their depths and then retreat into shadow. Alarm, probably, at him waking her like this, fully clothed, at such an early hour.

His tone apologetic, he broke the bad news to her. 'I have to fly to Geneva to see a client. It's a total pain, but I can't get out of it. I'm taking the earliest flight out.' He made a face. 'I'll be back in time for dinner, so... Look, have an easy day, OK? Lounge around the hotel or get the concierge to put a limo at your disposal. I'll see you this evening.'

He dropped another, even swifter kiss on her mouth, burningly conscious that he was cutting it very fine to make it to Fiumicino for his flight.

'Mi dispiace molto—'

And he was gone, striding out of the room, heading for the lift banks, wanting the flight over, the day over, and the evening to come, so he could get back to where he wanted to be.

Here.

With Connie.

For a long while Connie just lay there. Scarcely moving. Scarcely breathing. The room was deathly quiet, with not even the hum of the air-con to disturb the silence— for the temperature was dropping and it was no longer needed. But not heating yet, either.

It was poised between hot and cold.

Scalding hot and killing cold…
Like me.

She was poised between two overpowering impulses, completely contrary, that were tearing her in two.

Random thoughts were going through her head, almost like the wisps of a dream—not that she could remember dreaming last night.

But was that so surprising, given that her dreams had been completely shattered…obliterated…with a few simple words from Dante.

She heard them again now, in this 'in between' place where she seemed to be, with the room dim from the early hour and the drawn curtains, the air so quiet. Only the sound of her shallow breaths penetrated.

'Plenty of time…before we need to think about our divorce…'

They were repeating themselves on a loop. A loop she couldn't stop, or change, or get out of her head.

Such simple words. Such devastating consequences. Circling around and around in her head.

Round and round they went—like millstones, crushing her to pieces between them. Crushing her stupid, *stupid* dreams and all her hopes and secret longings. Grinding them all to dust…

She must have slept again, somehow, with the millstones grinding still, because when she surfaced again it was to the sound of the hotel phone beside her. She fumbled for the handset, barely awake. It was the reception desk, telling her she had a visitor.

She glanced at the time display—it was gone ten

in the morning, and bright sunlight was pressing behind the curtain drapes.

'Signor Ranieri is here, *signora*.'

She started. *Rafaello* was here?

Still hazy with heavy, comfortless sleep, she struggled to sit up.

'I'll… I'll be down shortly.'

She dropped the handset, staring blankly. What on earth was Rafaello doing here?

Her mobile phone pinged with a text, and she stared at it.

Connie, hi—I hope I'm not disturbing you. Dante asked me to look in on you since he had to abandon you at short notice. I'm at your disposal for the day if you like. Ciao. R

She swallowed. Part of her wanted to text back and tell him to go away. She could not cope with him. Could not cope with anything at all.

But I have to!

She stared bleakly into the luxurious bedroom, so handsomely appointed, from the velvet window drapes to the huge carved wooden bed and the ornate carpets. It seemed alien, so entirely alien.

She threw back the bedclothes, stumbled up, her mind in pieces, her thoughts in pieces…ground down to dust.

Dante's plane was touching down in Geneva—the last place he wanted to be. Because the only place he wanted to be was back in Rome. With Connie.

Maybe I should have brought her with me. She could have had the day in Geneva while I got my business meeting over and done with and then—who knows?—we could have spent the night here, and flown back to Rome tomorrow?

That way she'd have been with him on the flight there and back, and he wouldn't be missing her the way he was right now.

It had seemed so wrong to leave her like that. OK, so he'd left her during the day in Milan, when he went into the office, but that wasn't the same thing as flying off to a different country without her—even if he was going to be back in time for dinner.

As he waited for the plane to draw to a standstill so they could disembark, he quickly texted her.

Missing you already. I've asked Raf to come and keep you company. See you tonight. I will text when I know what flight I can make. The earliest I can!

He ended it with a line of smiley faces, which would make her smile too, he knew, and then slid his phone away, seized up his briefcase and levered himself from his seat to get off the plane as soon as he could.

The sooner he was in Geneva, the sooner he could see his client, and the sooner he could turn right around and get back to the airport again.

Back with Connie.

The only place he wanted to be.

* * *

'Connie...'

Rafaello's greeting was friendly as he came towards her in the hotel's opulent lobby. But when he reached her, he stopped. Scrutinised her.

Concern filled his face. 'You look as white as a sheet,' he said.

He took her elbow, guided her into the nearby lounge. It was possible to have breakfast there, seated in comfortable armchairs with low tables between, overlooking the glorious gardens. But it wasn't busy, and he headed for a pair of armchairs away from the other occupants.

She sat down, as limp as a rag doll.

'What's happened?' Rafaello asked quietly as he took his seat opposite her.

She looked at him. Her face wasn't working properly, she knew.

'I don't know what to do,' she said finally. The words fell from her like stones.

Rafaello's level gaze rested on her. 'In what respect?' he pressed when she went silent again.

'Dante,' she said. And his name, too, fell like a stone.

Rafaello crossed one leg over the other. 'Ah...' he said.

A waiter was hovering, and Rafaello turned to Connie.

'Have you had breakfast?'

She shook her head numbly.

'Then you should,' he said.

He ordered food for her, and coffee for himself, and the waiter disappeared.

Connie swallowed. There was a huge stone in her throat and needles in her lungs. She became aware that Rafaello was speaking and looked at him. He had that lawyer look about him and his eyes were resting on her, their expression guarded.

'It was what he said at dinner last night, wasn't it?' he said.

Her eyes widened, stared, then dropped away.

She heard Rafaello's voice continuing. 'You understood what he told Bianca?'

She could only nod numbly. What use to deny it? None.

'He…he confirmed it when I asked him about it later…in our room. He said he'd told her we weren't married. At first I didn't understand why he'd said that to her…'

She lifted her heavy gaze to Rafaello—his face was impassive, unreadable.

'And then…then he…he explained. Oh, not in relation to Bianca. But what he said about us. About him. About…' she swallowed, and it hurt to swallow over the stone in her throat '…me.'

'And what did Dante say about you?' he asked.

She shouldn't tell him. It was private, wasn't it? And Rafaello had never approved of his friend's marriage in the first place, so he would agree with Dante anyway. He'd be glad to hear it.

But she couldn't *not* say it.

Because it filled her head and her lungs and her consciousness.

'He said…he said that he respected that I had my own life to lead, and that although he'd prefer to keep our marriage going for another few months, to be on the safe side, I must not feel any…any obligation to stay in Italy with him for all that time…that I could head back to the UK whenever I wanted.'

The stone in her throat was harder and larger than ever. It was suffocating her now.

'And then…then he said there was plenty of time before we had to think about our…our divorce…'

She fell silent. Her mouth was as dry as dust. Her eyes sank again, too heavy to keep looking at Rafaello. She didn't want to. She didn't want to see what expression might be on the face of Dante's friend, who had never wanted him to marry her at all—for any length of time or for any purpose.

For a moment there was silence. Then she heard Rafaello speak, calmly and dispassionately.

'Well, he has spoken his mind, and now you know where you stand. Ah…here is your breakfast. While you eat, you must tell me what you plan to do now.'

Connie drew a breath. It was painful. Her throat was tight and she felt weak as a kitten, with incoherent thoughts whirring in her head like a swarm of flies.

The waiter was setting out her breakfast—orange juice, hot fragrant coffee, freshly baked *cornetti* and delicate pats of butter and pots of apricot jam. She didn't want to eat, but knew she must. She had no strength in her. None at all.

Rafaello poured coffee for them both and sat back, his cup in his hand, crossing his legs in a relaxed fashion. As she ate, forcing herself to swallow slowly but steadily, he kept silent, but he was still looking at her, she knew.

She finished her *cornetti*, then looked back at him... Dante's friend. 'You never wanted him to marry me, did you?' she said tiredly.

He paused before answering. Then: 'I thought it very...risky. You were strangers to each other—complete strangers. And he was running on anger at the time, and that's never a good aid to wise decisions. But since then...' He paused again, and now he was frowning slightly. 'Since then you seem to have worked things out between you. I'd hoped—'

He broke off, taking a breath.

His voice was gentle when he said, 'Connie, what do you intend to do now?'

She forced herself to speak. To say what she dreaded having to say. She had tried to deny the need to say anything, but no longer could. She had to face saying the words.

'I have to leave him,' she said.

The words fell into a heavy silence.

'I think,' Rafaello said eventually, 'that is the right decision. For both of you.'

His eyes rested on her but she could read nothing in them. They were as inscrutable as any lawyer's.

'But I also think you should do one more thing,' he added.

She stared at him dully. She was breaking up inside and it was agony.

'What…what thing?' she asked, her lips numb.

And Rafaello told her.

Dante stared at the text on his phone, frowning as the taxi edged through the traffic in Geneva, en route to his client's hotel.

Dante, ciao. Connie wasn't at the Falcone—looks like she's headed into the city on her own.

Immediately, he texted Connie.

Sorry to hear you missed Raf. Have fun in Rome. What are you going to be seeing?

He didn't get an answer before the taxi pulled up and he had to go into his meeting. But when he emerged a couple of hours later there was still no reply from Connie. He frowned again.

Hi—how are you doing? My meeting's finished and I'm in with a chance of making an earlier flight back to Rome. I can meet you in town, or back at the Falcone. You choose.

He didn't get a reply to that either.

He texted Raf. Not wanting to, but feeling an edge

of anxiety. Rome was safe enough, but maybe Connie had been mugged for her phone? These things happened.

Raf knew nothing, and told him so. He said he would text Connie as well, to let her know Dante was trying to get in touch.

Next Dante phoned the Falcone, to see if Connie had got back there safely. But she hadn't.

His frown deepened. So did his level of anxiety.

Repeated texts to Connie got no response. Fear bit at him, warring with reason.

She was OK—of course she was OK! Maybe her phone was dead. Maybe she just wasn't checking it. Maybe…

He was on board his flight, waiting for take-off, when a text finally arrived from her.

Dante, I'm so sorry—I'm back in England. I've heard there's a chance of getting on a Master's course at very short notice, so I thought I should go for it! I'm sorry to cut short our fabulous holiday, but perhaps it's for the best. Time to get on with our own lives— they've been on hold long enough.

The text ended with kisses—four of them. That was all.

A flight attendant was coming by, checking seat belts. Dante stopped her progress.

'I need to get off this flight immediately.' His voice was urgent, imperative.

'I am so sorry, but that isn't possible now.' The flight attendant was polite, but adamant.

He sat back, closing his eyes in frustration.

But also in so much more than that.

Connie let herself into her cottage. It was dark already. The coach from Heathrow had only taken her to Taunton. She'd had to change to a local bus to the village, and then get a taxi here. Exhaustion filled her—but it was not of the body.

The cottage was cold and bleak and it smelt fusty, having been empty for so long. Slowly, numbly, she went around putting on the lights, picking up the pile of post that had accumulated since Mrs Bowen, who had keys, had last done so on her behalf, and dumping it on the table, where the rest of it was neatly stacked.

She went into the kitchen, flicked the heating on. She wouldn't light a fire—she had no energy for it. She had no energy for anything. No will for anything. Except to crawl up to her room, get under her duvet, and sob her stupid heart out.

But what was the point of doing that? None.

Bleakly, she stared into the little living room. This was where Dante had proposed to her. Proposed a bizarre marriage of mutual convenience. He would get something he wanted. She would get something she wanted. It had been equal. Fair. A perfectly balanced contract. Win-win for both of them.

And it had worked. Worked while Gran was alive… worked while Connie was the way she'd been when they had tied the knot: lumpy, frumpy and dumpy.

But then…

Then I went off contract.

And that had changed everything between them.

She shut her eyes in misery.

Because I just could not resist taking the chance of making my wildest fantasy come true.

The fantasy of having the most fabulous man in the world look at her with an expression in his eyes that was not friendliness, or pleasantness, or even, after her grandmother's death, sympathy and concern.

She had wanted what she had never thought she would ever see in his eyes.

Desire.

And when that magical moment had come, and Dante had indeed looked at her with desire in his dark, gold-flecked eyes, and taken her into his arms to make her his, it had been so much more blissful than she had imagined.

And there had been more—so much more to her fantasy. And it had only grown stronger and stronger with every day she'd spent with Dante in Italy. Those days in Milan…him going off to his office, she to the market, to buy ingredients for their dinner, preparing things, cooking with him…

Like a proper married couple—a real married couple…

Because that, in the end, had been her ultimate fantasy, hadn't it? To settle down with Dante in married domestic bliss.

It was what her parents had had. She knew that from her own memories and from what her grandmother had told her. For her parents it had been cut tragically short, but for herself and for Dante she had hoped—oh, how she had hoped—that they would be given what her parents had not had. What Dante's own parents—however they'd lived their lives—had not had either.

But instead...

Dante never wanted that! Never wanted it at all! Not with me.

She gave a smothered cry and turned away, unable to bear looking at where Dante had sat, offering her the means to keep Gran at home, lifting her crushing money worries from her.

And all she'd had to do was sign her name on a marriage certificate...

For a limited time only.

That stone in her throat was back again, and she could not breathe.

A truth so harsh, so cruel, so brutal, was slamming into her, taking the air from her lungs.

I thought his desire for me would change that—would make him want our marriage to be real for the rest of our lives...

Bitterness filled her mouth.

It was not his fault. It was hers and hers alone.

Mine only.

And she would have to live with it for the rest of her life.

A life without Dante.

CHAPTER NINE

Dante was in the office, working. He was poring over the complex investment plan which one of his financial analysts had prepared for a particularly demanding client. He needed to give it his full attention, but that seemed impossible right now. His brain wouldn't focus. Not on pages of figures and graphs and lists of potential shareholdings and loans.

There was only one thing his brain could focus on.

Connie.

And she was not with him any longer.

Why?

That was the question burning a hole in his brain. OK, so she'd said she wanted to apply for a Master's. But couldn't she have done that from Italy? Everything was online these days; she could easily have applied remotely. And if she'd been offered an interview she could have flown back to the UK for a few days—hell, he'd have gone with her. They could have looked in on the cottage, caught a few days in London…

But no, she'd upped sticks and gone. Just like that.

When we still had months left to be together.

His face tensed. But if she got on this damned course they wouldn't have months to be together, would they?

Her time here, with me, will be over.

It was like a punch to his guts.

But it was absolutely nothing like the punch that came when his PA came through his door and carefully, knowing how black his mood was, placed in front of him a sealed package that had just arrived by air courier from London.

Numbly, he tore it open and yanked out the documents within. And then, as if all the breath had been forced from him by a paralysing blow, he stared in shock at what they told him.

Connie sat on the train, staring out of the window at the sodden countryside, the leafless trees. Autumn was fast turning into winter, and the weather was miserable. She pulled her coat around her, wriggled her feet in her boots. It wasn't her old winter coat, nor were they her old winter boots, but when she'd gone to stock up on winter clothes she'd been modest in her purchasing.

Memory plucked at her, of Dante taking her shopping in the fabled Quadrilatero in Milan. Of wandering blissfully, wonderingly, in and out of the famous fashion houses. Dante had spent a fortune on her...

Well, she would have no use for those fabulous clothes now. She'd left them all behind—even the ones she'd taken to Rome. She hoped he'd be able to sell them…they must be worth a huge amount, even second hand.

Her mind skittered away. She did not want to think about it—did not want to think about Dante. Because there was no point. Not any longer.

She felt misery clutch at her, bleak and desolate. She missed him so much.

How could she face the rest of her life—decades and decades and decades—without him?

You have to—that's all there is to it.

And if she'd yielded to temptation that terrible morning—to stay with Dante even after what he'd revealed to her, to stay with him every single day she could until he decided it was safe to divorce her—when that time had come it would have been an even greater agony to leave him!

No, nightmare though it had been, she'd had to do what she had done. Leave him that very morning.

She felt her throat constrict even more as she remembered what Rafaello had said to her in his calm, lawyerlike way on that hideous morning when she had decided she must leave Dante. Even if she could not yet divorce him.

Rafaello had argued otherwise.

'You should not believe, Connie, that you must prolong your marriage any further. Divorcing Dante immediately, on the grounds of irretrievable breakdown, would not invalidate the terms of his grandfather's will because it is, after all, quite true…is it not?'

A stifled sob broke from her.

Irretrievable breakdown—

Those words were like weights, crushing her— crushing all those hopes and dreams that she had once so stupidly believed in.

I believed that what I wanted was what Dante wanted too! That he would want what we had together to last for ever. But he never did want it to last—never intended it to last. For him, it was always going to end—always!

She gave another smothered cry, thankful that the train was not crowded, that she had a no one near her to witness her misery. There was only the sodden landscape passing her by outside, as bleak and bare as the landscape of her mind and her heart.

She hadn't wanted to come to London today, but Rafaello had said it was necessary. This next stage of the divorce was not something that could be done virtually, he'd told her. It had to be face to face.

She'd wanted to use a local West Country lawyer, but Rafaello had said that, given Dante was Italian, and she had signed a prenup, and his financial resources were so vast compared with hers, only a London lawyer of sufficient calibre would do. Fortunately Rafaello was personally acquainted with just such a suitable lawyer, and she had gone along with his recommendation.

In a remote way she was grateful to Rafaello for taking charge...guiding her through the whole hideous process with his legal expertise. It was kind of him—he must be feeling sorry for her.

But maybe he's only doing it for Dante—to free him from me as quickly as he can.

And now the tears she had been trying not to shed spilled from her. Tears from the agonising pain of knowing that Dante—the man she had married as a stranger, who had become her friend, kind and compassionate, and then her lover, desiring and passionate, the man she had woven her stupid, delusional dreams over—had never wanted her to be the wife she had come to long to be with all her heart.

Never.

Dante sat on the plane, his expression closed. But thoughts were crowding into his head. He was keeping them all crammed down under a heavy weight. It was essential he do so.

Memory pierced him of how he'd driven down to the West Country, fury in his heart, to seek out Rafaello at that damn wedding and demand he find a way to get him out of the trap his grandfather had sprung on him.

His anger had been paramount, all-consuming. Was it anger in him now, storming beneath that heavy weight he was crushing his thoughts with? He didn't know. Wasn't going to look. He was simply going to go on staring at the document in his hand, taken out of the briefcase beside him.

The petition for divorce.

And the letter that had arrived since from Connie's London lawyer, requesting a meeting.

'Connie—how are you?'

Rafaello's greeting was courteous as he came forward to meet her. She'd arrived by taxi from Paddington

Station to an elegant eighteenth-century townhouse in the Inns of Court, the premises of the law firm Rafaello had recommended, and he had been waiting for her in the narrow lobby.

She swallowed as he shook her hand. It was hard to see him again, even though she was grateful for his support through this whole agonising business. He helped her off with her coat, and came with her as she was shown upstairs to a wood-panelled office, where she was introduced to the senior partner to whom she had only spoken virtually so far.

He got to his feet behind an old-fashioned mahogany desk. 'Ah, Mrs Cavelli—how good to finally meet you in person.'

Numbly, she returned his handshake, took the chair Rafaello drew up for her. She felt frozen all over, inside and out.

'What...what happens next?' she asked.

The man resumed his seat and looked at her in a kindly fashion over the rim of his spectacles.

'Well, as you know, your husband has been served with your petition. You were married in the United Kingdom, so that is good—it keeps things simpler. However, your husband being an Italian citizen adds a degree of complication...as I believe you already appreciate.'

He nodded at Rafaello who, sitting beside her, said, 'But not to a great degree, as I have explained to you.'

She looked bleakly at him, and then the senior partner.

'I just want it done as quickly as possible with the minimum fuss.' Her voice was low and strained, as her fingers knotted in her lap over her handbag.

'Of course. Very understandable...' said the lawyer, nodding in agreement. 'Very well, let us continue—'

The phone on his desk suddenly rang, and with a murmured apology to Connie he picked it up.

He listened a moment. Then: 'Thank you. Yes, right away, if you please.'

He replaced the handset and looked across at Connie. His expression was unreadable.

And so, she realised with a sudden stab of alarm in her breast, was Rafaello's.

Through the oak door of the office she heard rapid footsteps, and then the door was unceremoniously pushed open.

Dante strode in.

He stopped dead. A man, middle-aged, bespectacled, was getting to his feet, politely greeting him. Dante ignored him. He had eyes for one person in the room, and one only.

His wife.

His wife, upon whose shoulder Rafaello Ranieri's hand was pressing.

All the emotions that had been hammered down so ruthlessly on his journey here smashed through.

Rage ignited.

Explosively.

'Get your hands off my wife!'

A shocked sound came from the man behind the desk.

'Mr Cavelli! If you please!'

Dante ignored him. Ignored everything but the sight of Rafaello touching Connie.

Rage came again.

'It's you, isn't it? You're the one who's stirred all this up! Well, damn you! Do you hear me? Damn you to hell!'

He was speaking Italian now, and anger was boiling from him. He saw Rafaello getting to his feet, holding up a hand, his other hand still pressing down on Connie's shoulder.

'Dante—cool it.'

His words were perfectly calm—which enraged Dante all the more.

He started forward. He wanted to knock Raf's hand off Connie's shoulder, and then he wanted to knock him out cold.

A cry stopped him in his tracks. Connie had jolted to her feet, dislodging Rafaello's hand with the movement.

Dante's rage turned. Turned on her.

'Just what the *hell* is all this about?'

He'd gone into English now, but his anger was just as searing in that language as in his own.

'You walk out on me without a word—without a single damn word you just walk out and disappear, high-tail it back to the UK on some totally spurious pretext—and next thing I get petitioned for *divorce*? What the *hell*?'

Rafaello spoke again. In English. 'Why the surprise, Dante? You were always going to get divorced, weren't you? Connie's just accelerated the procedure, that's all.'

His voice was still cool and calm. And it still enraged Dante.

'Shut your damn mouth, Raf! This is your doing! You've put Connie up to this! Though God knows why—or how!'

His eyes flashed back to Connie. With the small part of his brain that wasn't in total meltdown he saw that she was as white as a sheet.

He opened his mouth to speak, his anger even blacker. Because of course it was anger—what else could this all-consuming, overpowering emotion be?

But her pale, drawn face was twisting, her hand was flying to her mouth, stifling another cry torn from her, and then she was stumbling past him, pulling open the door, hurtling from the room.

Running from him.

She was gasping, no air in her lungs, as she pounded down the stairs. Only one thought possessed her. To get away…

The shock of Dante's arrival—the horror of his rage at her… She couldn't bear it. She couldn't bear it a moment longer, not for a second…

Her coat was hanging on a hook in the lobby and she grabbed at it, pushing her arms into the sleeves, fumbling with her handbag as she did so, yanking open the front door.

Behind her she could hear voices full of consternation, footsteps running down the stairs behind her.

She could hear her name being called—urgent, angry. In a flurry of desperation she started blindly down the short flight of stone steps leading to the pavement, still trying to thrust her right hand into her coat sleeve.

She felt her heel catch on the lowest step, tried to grab the railing. But her hand was not free. She felt herself being impelled forward, knowing in a moment of utter panic that she was falling…could not stop herself. Could not stop the pavement slamming up towards her, the lamppost smashing into her head as she fell, with a sickening thud, on the rock-hard, merciless paving stones.

'Connie!'

Dante's voice was hoarse with horror and he was there in an instant, crouched down beside her. He cried her name again, but she did not move.

In terror, he lifted his shaking hand to her throat. His eyes closed in abject relief and he breathed again. There was a pulse.

But blood was seeping through her hair, trickling onto her forehead.

'Get an ambulance!' he demanded.

Then Raf was there, crouched down too, his phone in his hand, jabbing out the emergency number, demanding an ambulance immediately.

Dante grabbed the phone from him. *'Now!'* he yelled into it.

And then he was trying to lift Connie, attempting to get his arm under her shoulder.

Rafaello's hand clamped down on him with all its weight, restraining him.

'*No!* It's a head injury—and maybe her neck, too. You are not to move her—not even a centimetre!'

Dante still wanted to punch Rafaello, but he lifted his arm away. Other people were there now. Connie's lawyer, the woman who had shown him in. All were expressing their concern. Connie herself was not stirring.

Numbly, Dante kept his fingers at her throat, on the thin, frail pulse still beating there.

And as her blood trickled slowly over her chalk-white cheek onto his hand, as he knelt on the pavement beside her, words formed in his head, carving into him, one by one.

Her blood is on my hands…

The ambulance came. Scooped Connie up and drove off with her, blue lighting through the traffic.

Rafaello hailed a taxi, piling Dante into it, but by the time they reached the hospital Connie had been rushed away.

Dante strode up to the reception desk in A&E, numb with dread.

'My wife,' he said curtly. 'She's just been brought in. Unconscious. Head wound. Where is she?

His questions were staccato, demanding. His face looked like stone.

The receptionist checked, conferred with a colleague, then looked at him.

'She's in X-Ray,' she said. 'She needs a CT scan.

They'll know more soon. Could you please fill out this form with her personal details?'

Dante ignored the form and headed for the seating area closest to the door that said *X-Ray and Imaging*.

It opened, and a man in a white coat with a stethoscope around his neck walked through.

Dante stepped in front of him.

'My wife,' he said urgently. 'She fell. Unconscious. Head injury. Bleeding—'

The doctor glanced at him for a moment, then nodded, gave a tired smile. He didn't always get to give good news, but this was one time he could.

'She'll be OK,' he said.

Dante's eyes closed, and emotion drenched through every fibre of his being.

CHAPTER TEN

THERE WAS A mist in the room. Connie could see it. Feel it. It was all around her. Inside her. Blurring her vision. Blurring everything.

She tried to blink, to clear it, but it would not go. The mist was covering up her thoughts, her feelings, and she could not get through it to find them, even though she had a feeling it was very important that she do so. The effort was hideous, and with a low moan in her throat she gave in…giving herself up to the mist.

When she next surfaced the mist had gone—not completely, but it was only around the edges of the room now, blurring the walls and the edges of her brain, blurring the edges of her thoughts, her feelings.

Those thoughts and feelings had come into sharp, agonising focus. Each one edged with a knife blade like a razor.

Dante. Dante in front of her like an avenging god of old, denouncing her.

Misery filled her, piercing the edges of the mist. Misery and so much more.

The door was opening and a nurse came in. 'How are you feeling?' she asked brightly.

'Groggy,' said Connie.

The nurse nodded. 'That's to be expected. But you'll be glad to know you're doing very well. We'll keep you in for observation, but all the signs are looking good, so you should be OK to go home before too long.'

She went on with her checks and Connie just lay there inertly. When the nurse had finished, she looked down at Connie.

'Your husband's *very* keen to come in and see you—do you think you're up to it?'

Connie's stomach hollowed.

'No,' she said.

She shut her eyes, the lids suddenly as heavy as lead, and sleep took her. A blessed relief.

Dante was pacing. Pacing up and down the wide, carpeted corridor outside Connie's room. He'd had her moved to the private wing of the hospital, into a room of her own.

Further down the corridor, in a wide area that was provided with comfortable chairs, Rafaello was seated, reading one of the newspapers provided. He was still as calm as Dante was agitatedly restless.

'The doctors say she is fine, Dante,' he said, and not for the first time. 'She was concussed, but the scans are clear. She needs rest, and observation, and some pain meds.'

Dante ignored him. He went back to pacing. Up, and then down. Up and then down.

Connie, so close, just the other side of a door, might as well have been on the far side of the moon.

Connie was sitting up. She felt frail, but that was all. She was on painkillers, still wired up so the medics could check her blood oxygen and whatever else they wanted to keep an eye on, but other than that she was OK.

Or so they kept telling her.

It was a lie, of course.

How could she be OK?

How can I be OK ever again?

The nurse finished her latest round of checks and readings, then smiled brightly at Connie.

'If I don't let that husband of yours in soon,' she said, 'he's likely to tear the door off its hinges! Can I let him in, finally?'

Connie shut her eyes, the way she had last time, but this time blessed sleep did not come to her rescue.

'I'll take that as a yes,' said the nurse. And there was more than a touch of humour in her voice as she said, heading towards the door, 'I can tell you now: if I had a husband who looked like that I'd have him right in here holding my hand!'

She gave an extravagant sigh and went out.

Connie heard her saying, 'You can go in now, Mr Cavelli. But not for very long. Your wife is still very tired.'

Connie heard the deep sound of Dante's voice answering the nurse, and then he was thrusting open the door and striding in. But she was busy—very busy—keeping her eyes tight shut.

She felt his shadow fall over her, felt his presence. Heard him speak her name. His voice was low, strained, hesitant. Not the harsh anger that she had been expecting.

'How…how are you feeling?'

She wanted to keep her eyes closed. Wanted sleep to claim her, or oblivion in any form, but knew she could not avoid him for ever.

She opened her eyes and he was there, in her vision instantly. Standing by her bed, so tall and so dark against the light.

'We…we have to talk,' she heard him say.

His voice was still quiet and a little hoarse. His face worked, and she saw emotion flashing across it. Incomprehension.

'Connie—*why* did you leave me? Leave me when you did?'

Her eyes slid away from him. It was impossible to tell him the truth.

'It…it was just as Rafaello said. We were always going to get divorced. I just…like he said…accelerated it…'

It was all she could get out.

'But *why*? Connie—why then? What happened? I don't understand! We were so *good* together, and we were having such a wonderful time. It was like a non-stop holiday. So *why*—?'

He broke off. She'd heard the total incomprehension in his voice. It matched the look on his face. Like a knife in her heart, it told her everything that she already knew. Had known since he'd clearly spelt it out to her on that last unbearable night in Rome. Spelt out just why all her stupid dreams had been just that.

Something was changing in his face. Something hard, and edged like a blade.

'Is this to do with Raf?' He stood there, looking down at her. Eyes like knives. 'Egging you on. Resting his hand on your shoulder like he has a right to touch you.'

She was staring at him. Staring at him with an incomprehension in her face that outdid even his.

'Raf…?' she breathed. 'You think *Raf*—?'

She broke off, not even capable of putting into words what Dante was implying.

'Maybe that's why he's so keen on you getting divorced ASAP! So *he* can move in on you!'

Her face worked. She tried to speak, but couldn't. What could she say? What could she possibly say to that?

She saw emotion flash again across Dante's face. A different one this time. Vehement and possessive.

'Well, he can take a hike! I won't let him near you! Because you're mine, Connie! *Mine!* My wife!'

She felt her face start to crumple.

'Don't say that, Dante. Don't say it. It doesn't mean anything!' She took a breath…a rasping one. 'We both know why we married—it got us what we wanted. You got your inheritance and I got security for my grandmother.' She shut her eyes. 'That was all we wanted...'

'To getting what we want.'

The words of his toast as they'd drunk champagne to celebrate their wedding on the private jet stabbed in her head again.

True for him. But, oh, not for me—not for me! Because I have come to want so much more! Something that he cannot give me—can never give me...

Anguish filled her...possessed her utterly.

There was silence. Silence all around her.

Then she heard Dante speak. Slowly. Heavily.

'That isn't actually true.'

She heard him breathe in, then go on.

'It stopped being true that night in London. When you walked into that cocktail bar and knocked the breath from my lungs.'

She shook her head, eyes still shut. 'No,' she said.

She opened her eyes, looked right at him before she spelt out the truth that it had cost her so dearly to discover...to face up to.

'What has been between us since that night,' she said, speaking slowly, carefully, every word a blade on her skin, 'has nothing to do with marriage. It was simply...simply an affair.'

She had known that since that last dreadful night in Rome. An affair was all that Dante had wanted from her. That was the truth that had made a mockery of her hopes and dreams. She'd wanted to make their marriage a real one—had thought that was what was happening between them. But it wasn't. Because all

Dante had wanted from the moment she'd walked into that cocktail bar and seen desire flare in his eyes— desire for *her,* the woman he'd made himself marry to get his inheritance—was an affair.

An affair to while away the time until he could safely divorce her, as he'd always intended. Until he could part company with her. Get his life back.

'It was all you ever wanted,' she said now. 'An affair. And now I've called time on it.'

Dante heard her words. They hung in the air between them as she looked at him, so pale, propped up on the hospital pillows. There was a dressing on her head where she'd smashed into the lamppost. A drip in her arm. She was wired up to a monitor. An oxygen meter on her finger.

I could have lost her today.

The words rang in his head. Just as they had when he'd seen her fall, seen her lying on the payment. Unconscious. Bleeding.

Her blood is on my hands.

He felt emotions rise in him like a river, a tide, an ocean. Flowing together, coming together, surging in his veins.

Slowly, he began to speak. Feeling for each word, placing one after another so carefully. And all the while that great tide of emotion was sweeping around his body, forcing out those words that rose to his lips.

It was impossible not to speak. It was essential that he speak. As essential as air to breathe and water to drink and food to eat… Essential to his very existence.

Each word was distinct, coming, it seemed, from very far away—from a place that no longer existed nor ever could again.

'You know that when I married you, Connie, I bitterly resented having to do so. Having to marry at all! Having my hand forced by my grandfather. Being controlled by him from beyond the grave the way he'd controlled me in life. I wanted only two things from my marriage to you—to get my inheritance and then to end that marriage.'

He frowned.

'What I said to you, Connie, that last evening in Rome, was completely true. For all that I never wanted to marry, you had proved to be an absolute Trojan. I appreciated you so much. You'd accepted everything on the terms I wanted. Everything.'

He stopped, tried to look at her, but wasn't seeing her.

'Even after you came back from that health resort looking so incredible…even after that you still accepted everything on my terms. And I realised I could have it all. I could have you, so warm and lovely and irresistible. I could have you and I could still, when the time was right, have my freedom back. Courtesy of our divorce.'

His expression changed. Became troubled.

'That was why I was so adamant that no one knew of our marriage. I didn't want wedding rings, or you changing your name, or even for you to meet any of my friends—except Raf, who knew all about you anyway. I didn't want you to be my wife in more than name only—because I didn't want a wife at all.'

His frown deepened. Suddenly it felt as if a stiletto were being slipped into his ribs—intangible on impact, but deadly in effect…

'But when you left me the day I flew to Geneva… when it was *you* filing for divorce…it was then I realised how completely and totally meaningless it had been to want my life back.'

He felt emotion soar from some deep place inside himself he had never known existed. A place that was suddenly blazing with light. With clarity. With truth.

'Because you *were* my life, Connie. And I knew that without you I had no life. There would be no life worth living without you in it.'

He saw her face work…her beautiful deep blue eyes fill with diamond tears. But she did not speak or move.

So he did. Lowering himself to sit on her bed, he took her hand—the hand that had never had his ring upon its finger, nor put one on his, anticipating the day when he'd get his own life back and be free again.

But I shall never be free—for freedom would only be loss. The loss of all that is most precious to me.

He felt her fingers press into his, heard her try to speak, and then he was lifting her hand to his mouth, bringing it to his lips, holding it fast. He lowered it, closing his other hand around it so that both her hands were held tightly, so very tightly, between his.

It was as if his very life depended on it. The life

he wanted—the only life would ever want now that he could see, could know, the truth of it…

'No life worth living,' he said again.

And he was seeing her now—who she was and what she was and what she would *always* be to him.

'No life worth living without the woman I love.'

A cry came from her as if torn from deep inside her. The diamond tears in her eyes spilled over.

'I'd begun to hope that you had started to feel for me what I was feeling for you,' she said. 'I wanted so badly to believe that you had come to think of me as a real wife—a wife for ever…'

Her tears were coursing down her cheeks. Tears he had caused. Tears he would never let her shed over him again. Emotion was pouring through him, rich and warm and golden. Filling every cell in his body.

He bent forward, kissing her tear-wet eyes, and then, in tender homage, grazed her soft, trembling lips with his.

It was, without doubt, the sweetest, most precious moment in all the world.

How could I have not known? How could I have not seen? Not realised what was happening day after day? Night after night? Not known how precious she is to me?

It seemed extraordinary to him now. Extraordinary and unbelievable. That he had gone on thinking for so long that the original reasons why they had married still had anything at all to do with what was between them now…

He lifted his mouth away from hers, his eyes pouring golden love into the beautiful blue ones that were lifted to his with an expression of wonder in them that made his heart turn over until he felt breathless.

He gave a smile. A crooked smile. Pressed her hands fast between his. Holding them against his heart, which from this moment on would beat for her and her alone.

Then a regretful expression appeared in his eyes. He shook his head in rueful self-castigation. 'You know,' he said, and there was sincere remorse in his voice as eyes poured gold into hers, '*la mia amata moglie*—my most beloved—you're going to have to face having a husband who, for all his financial savvy, is absolutely, shamefully and extraordinarily stupid.'

A voice spoke from the doorway. 'I will second that,' said Rafaello.

Dante's head whipped round. Rafaello was lounging against the doorjamb, perusing the scene. Dante was about to speak, but Rafaello's attention was on Connie now.

'He's an idiot,' he said, with a smile in his voice, 'and I've had to go to quite ridiculous lengths to get him to finally realise it—shocking him into it with the threat of the divorce I urged you to pursue, Connie.'

His smile deepened.

'But for all his idiocy and blindness in not realising that you were the one he must keep and cherish all his life, he's still my friend.' He levered himself away from the doorjamb. 'And if he hasn't told you yet that he loves you just as much as it is obvious to me that you love him—well, then, he's an even bigger idiot than I think him already!'

Dante threw him a dagger glance, but this time it had no real blade in it. 'Raf, get out!' he said warningly, but in a friendly fashion.

Rafaello threw up a hand. 'I only looked in to tell you the nurse says five minutes longer and no more.'

He retreated, closing the door behind him. Dante turned his attention back to Connie. The only place he wanted it to be—would only ever want it to be.

He pressed her hands. 'Five minutes, hmm…? Well, I think I can do it in that time.'

He bent forward, dropping down on to one knee but never for an instant letting go of Connie's hand. He thought he would never let it go again, for all his days.

He lowered his mouth to Connie's knuckles, which seemed to tremble at his touch. And as he lifted his mouth away his eyes pinned hers, blazing with golden light.

'You stole into my heart, Connie, and I didn't even know you were doing it. Your sweetness of nature, your devotion to your grandmother, the way I could talk to you, relax with you, be myself with you… You were becoming important to me, but I never realised just how much. And then, when you came to London and I saw just how beautiful you are, I wanted to sweep you away with me, into my arms, and keep you there. All those wonderful days and nights in Italy were so incredibly precious to me. The happiest time of my life—'

He broke off, emotion choking him.

Then: 'I want that happiness to be for ever. For you and for me. I want our marriage to be a real one.'

His grip on her hand tightened.

He took a breath and said what was in his heart. 'I proposed to you once, sitting in your grandmother's parlour, and you stared at me as if I were mad.' He gave a rueful twist of his mouth. 'Would you stare at me that way again if I proposed now?'

He saw the tears well in her eyes again, felt her hand tremble in his again.

He took it as a good sign.

And proposed to her all over again.

She heard his words. Heard his voice. Heard in both all that she'd longed to hear.

'I initially gave you many reasons for our marriage,' she heard him say, 'but now I give you only one.'

She saw his expression change, felt his clasp on her hand tighten. Emotion welled within her, and her fingers tightened on his in return.

Dante's eyes clung to hers. 'The reason I'm asking you to make your life with me, for ever and for always, is purely one abiding, eternal reason. For love.'

She leaned forward, kissed him on the mouth. His name broke from her, and it was apparently all he needed to hear, for his hand loosed hers and snaked around the nape of her neck, returning her kiss.

It was bliss, it was wonder, it was glory and it was happiness.

And above all it was love.

All that she had ever longed for.

And now possessed.

EPILOGUE

'THIS REALLY IS the most beautiful garden...' breathed Connie. 'The scent of the lavender is heavenly.' Her expression grew poignant. 'Like the lavender in Gran's cottage garden...'

She leant back into Dante's sheltering arms. The West Country cottage would always be there for them, but Connie had given the use of it to a charity that provided respite care for family carers in need of a break—and she knew her grandmother would have approved of that.

Their main home—hers and Dante's—was a spacious villa surrounded by gardens in the lush Lombardy countryside, within commuting distance of Milan for Dante.

Dante had kept his modern apartment for when they wanted to be in the city. Although... He smiled to himself. He was finding that country life was suiting him fine. Just fine.

And how should it not?

His arms wound around Connie—his adored, most precious Connie, the light of his life and the wonder of his heart. He stood with her there on the sunlit terrace, bathed in the warm Italian sun, with the heady scent of lavender all about them.

'She would be so very happy for me,' she said quietly.

Dante gave a wry laugh. 'And so, I know, would my grandfather for me. Everything he plotted and schemed for has come about.' His voice changed, became sad, regretful. 'I wish I had realised just why it was he put that clause in his will. I thought it was because he wanted to control me...the way he had controlled me all my life. But...' he took a difficult but necessary breath '...but now I know it was for a different reason. He wanted to protect me.'

He was silent for a moment, then spoke again.

'He wanted to protect me from having no one in my life. With my feckless parents gone, and with him gone too, he wanted me to have someone who was important to me. Someone who mattered. And for me to matter to someone in turn.'

Connie felt his arms tighten around her, and she pressed her own hands over his encircling ones.

'He gave me a gift I'd never realised I wanted,' he said, and now his mouth kissed her throat, soft and sensuous and blissfully possessive. 'A gift that is beyond price.'

She craned her head back, turning so that she could catch his lips with hers.

'As you are to me,' she said, her eyes aglow with all the love she felt for him, the love she would always feel. Her heart was overflowing with it.

For a while they stood there in total, absolute contentment, drinking in the scent of lavender, basking in the sunshine, Dante holding Connie close against him.

'When did Raf say he would be here?' she asked.

'Late afternoon,' Dante answered. He gave another wry laugh. 'I still resent that he could see so damnably clearly what was happening to me. That I was falling in love with you and didn't even know it myself!'

It was Connie's turn to laugh. 'Just as he could see that I was utterly in love with you.'

Dante made a face. 'All that needling—all that interference of his. For one purpose only. To get me to realise what you meant to me. He was baiting me about domestic bliss just to wake me up to the fact that that was exactly what I wanted!'

Connie turned in Dante's arms, winding her own around his neck and gazing up at him adoringly. 'And that is what we have, haven't we?' she said, love lighting up her eyes.

The same loving expression was in his own eyes as he looked down at her. 'Can you doubt it, Signora Cavelli, for one single, solitary second?'

She shook her head.

No, there were no doubts, and no possibility of doubts.

She felt her heart catch.

No possibility of anything except endless happiness.

All that she, and he, could ever want.

* * * * *

#4153 THE MAID'S PREGNANCY BOMBSHELL
Cinderella Sisters for Billionaires
by Lynne Graham

Shy hotel maid Alana is so desperate to clear a family debt that when she discovers Greek tycoon Ares urgently needs a wife, she blurts out a scandalous suggestion: *she'll* become his convenient bride. But as chemistry blazes between them, she has an announcement that will inconveniently disrupt his well-ordered world... She's having his baby!

#4154 A BILLION-DOLLAR HEIR FOR CHRISTMAS
by Caitlin Crews

When Tiago Villela discovers Lillie Merton is expecting, a wedding is nonnegotiable. To protect the Villela billions, his child must be legitimate. But his plan for a purely pragmatic arrangement is soon threatened by a dangerously insatiable desire...

#4155 A CHRISTMAS CONSEQUENCE FOR THE GREEK
Heirs to a Greek Empire
by Lucy King

Booking billionaire Zander's birthday is a triumph for caterer Mia. And the hottest thing on the menu? A scorching one-night stand! But a month later, he can't be reached. Mia finally ambushes him at work to reveal she's pregnant! He insists she move in with him, but this Christmas she wants all or nothing!

#4156 MISTAKEN AS HIS ROYAL BRIDE
Princess Brides for Royal Brothers
by Abby Green

Maddi hadn't fully considered the implications of posing as her secret half sister. *Or* that King Aristedes would demand she continue the pretense as his intended bride. Immersing herself in the royal life she was denied growing up is as compelling as it is daunting. But so is the thrill of Aristedes's smoldering gaze...

#4157 VIRGIN'S STOLEN NIGHTS WITH THE BOSS
Heirs to the Romero Empire
by Carol Marinelli
Polo player Elias rarely spares a glance for his staff, until he meets stable hand and former heiress Carmen. And their attraction is irresistible! Elias knows he'll give the innocent all the pleasure she could want, but that's it. Unless their passion can unlock a connection much harder to walk away from...

#4158 CROWNED FOR THE KING'S SECRET
Behind the Palace Doors...
by Kali Anthony
One year ago, her spine-tingling night with exiled king Sandro left Victoria pregnant and alone. Lied to by the palace, she believed he wanted nothing to do with them. So Sandro turning up on her doorstep—ready to claim her, his heir and his kingdom—is astounding!

#4159 HIS INNOCENT UNWRAPPED IN ICELAND
by Jackie Ashenden
Orion North wants Isla's company...and her! So when the opportunity to claim both at the convenient altar arises, he takes it. But with tragedy in his past, even their passion may not be enough to melt the ice encasing his heart...

#4160 THE CONVENIENT COSENTINO WIFE
by Jane Porter
Clare Redmond retreated from the world, pregnant and grieving her fiancé's death, never expecting to see his ice-cold brother, Rocco, again. She's stunned when the man who always avoided her storms back into her life, demanding they wed to give her son the life a Cosentino deserves!

HPCNMRB1023

Get 3 FREE REWARDS!

We'll send you 2 FREE Books <u>plus</u> a FREE Mystery Gift.

FREE Value Over **$20**

Both the **Harlequin®️ Desire** and **Harlequin Presents®️** series feature compelling novels filled with passion, sensuality and intriguing scandals.

YES! Please send me 2 FREE novels from the Harlequin Desire or Harlequin Presents series and my FREE gift (gift is worth about $10 retail). After receiving them, if I don't wish to receive any more books, I can return the shipping statement marked "cancel." If I don't cancel, I will receive 6 brand-new Harlequin Presents Larger-Print books every month and be billed just $6.30 each in the U.S. or $6.49 each in Canada, a savings of at least 10% off the cover price, or 3 Harlequin Desire books (2-in-1 story editions) every month and be billed just $7.83 each in the U.S. or $8.43 each in Canada, a savings of at least 12% off the cover price. It's quite a bargain! Shipping and handling is just 50¢ per book in the U.S. and $1.25 per book in Canada.* I understand that accepting the 2 free books and gift places me under no obligation to buy anything. I can always return a shipment and cancel at any time by calling the number below. The free books and gift are mine to keep no matter what I decide.

Choose one: ☐ **Harlequin Desire**
(225/326 BPA GRNA)

☐ **Harlequin Presents Larger-Print**
(176/376 BPA GRNA)

☐ **Or Try Both!**
(225/326 & 176/376 BPA GRQP)

Name (please print)

Address _____ Apt. #

City _____ State/Province _____ Zip/Postal Code

Email: Please check this box ☐ if you would like to receive newsletters and promotional emails from Harlequin Enterprises ULC and its affiliates. You can unsubscribe anytime.

Mail to the **Harlequin Reader Service:**
IN U.S.A.: P.O. Box 1341, Buffalo, NY 14240-8531
IN CANADA: P.O. Box 603, Fort Erie, Ontario L2A 5X3

Want to try 2 free books from another series! Call 1-800-873-8635 or visit www.ReaderService.com.

*Terms and prices subject to change without notice. Prices do not include sales taxes, which will be charged (if applicable) based on your state or country of residence. Canadian residents will be charged applicable taxes. Offer not valid in Quebec. This offer is limited to one order per household. Books received may not be as shown. Not valid for current subscribers to the Harlequin Presents or Harlequin Desire series. All orders subject to approval. Credit or debit balances in a customer's account(s) may be offset by any other outstanding balance owed by or to the customer. Please allow 4 to 6 weeks for delivery. Offer available while quantities last.

HDHP23

HARLEQUIN
PLUS

Try the best multimedia
subscription service for romance
readers like you!

Read, Watch and Play.

Experience the easiest way to get
the romance content you crave.

Start your **FREE TRIAL** at
<u>www.harlequinplus.com/freetrial</u>.